Killing Mister Oni
and other stories

J.B. Masaji

Copyright © 2022 Franklin Pass Press

All rights reserved.

ISBN: 978-0-9988554-1-7

Dedication

To the members of the El Paso Writer's League, for giving me the kick in the pants I needed to write.

Contents

Wolfsbane	1
Killing Mister Oni	18
180	32
THE SHADOWBEAR COMETH!!!	49
Running	68
Circles	79
trance	88
The Year of 100 Blind Dates	100

Author's Note

These stories were written between 2016 and 2021 for two writing contests: the El Paso Writer's League's annual Border Tapestry contest, and NYC Midnight's annual short fiction contest. These stories would not exist had it not been for the goal provided by those contests, and the professional critiques that I received from the judges regarding my submissions.

Wolfsbane

You have a memory from when you were barely two years old. Your developmental psychology professor told you this was impossible, that you must have heard about it when you were older and then convinced yourself you actually remembered it. But that can't be because the only person who was with you was your father, and he never talked about that moment.

This is the memory. You're riding in a car seat in the back of your father's beat-up '75 Civic, cold air piercing a gap in the window weathering and falling on your face. The car is surrounded on either side by impenetrable walls of trees, giant wooden fingers that stretch up towards the sky, grasping for something just out of reach.

It is night, and it is snowing. These aren't flurries like you get in El Paso but big, wet flakes falling in sheets like rain, sticking to the windshield as fast as the frantic wipers can push them away. The squeak of the wiper against the glass sounds like a pig squealing before slaughter. The sound is so loud you're afraid the wipers will snap under the weight, and then there will be nothing to protect the car from drowning under an ocean of snow.

The snow is falling fast, and the trees are crowding in to attack, and it's all so scary you start whimpering.

"Is everything okay Horatius?"

You nod, trying to look brave. Your father smiles at you through the rear view mirror.

"What sound does a wolf make?" your father asks.

You laugh, because in this memory your father asks you this as a game, a call and response, not as a form of catechesis.

"Come on Horatius, what sound does a wolf make?" he asks again.

"Aahooo!" you say, giggling.

"What's the call of the Chosen, Horatius?"

You lean your two year old head back, and you howl as loud as you can, drowning out the snow and the trees and the sputtering heater and the squealing windshield wiper blades.

"AAHOOO!!!"

On the first day of December, you fly home to El Paso for your grandfather's funeral. It's an unseasonably warm winter day. The heat greets you in the small gap of air between the airplane's door and the jet bridge.

Cindy worried about you leaving school this close to finals.

"I know he's your grandfather, Ray, but didn't you say you weren't close?" she said while holding a cup of coffee close to her chest. The steam from the coffee twirled around her face like smoke from a beat poet's cigarette.

You shivered slightly in the frigid Chicago air, wrapping the black scarf even tighter around your neck.

"He's not just my grandfather," you tried to explain. "He's an important figure in the community. Everyone in the neighborhood will be at the funeral." *Alpha*, you want to say. He's not just your grandfather, he's the Alpha of your pack, so you have to go back for his funeral. But you didn't say it because Cindy doesn't know what an Alpha is. She doesn't know you're Chosen, doesn't know she's an Other.

Your mother picks you up from the airport. She drives home along I-10, and you stare out the window, not talking. The city is bigger than when you left. The eastern edge of the city has been overrun by a horde of cookie cutter subdivisions that stretch out as far as the eye can see. Your mother turns into one of these cookie cutter subdivisions, every house just like the one next to it. This is where she lives now.

You meet your grandfather for the first time on your twelfth birthday. This was in the old house in Sunset Heights where you grew up.

You don't know anything is wrong. Your mother's hands tremble, but only a little, as she cuts a slice of moist chocolate cake and delicately lays it next to a scoop of mint chocolate chip ice cream. Your parents sing, and their combined voices drown out the sound of the summer monsoon rains outside. Your mother tenses when there is a knock at the door. She was expecting this.

When the door opens, your grandfather stands there. You recognize him from the single photo of her family your mother keeps on her dresser. In the photo your grandfather looks just like he does now. He wears a leather jacket, impossibly impractical for the summer heat, and his unkempt black hair falls just past his shoulders.

Your parents both stand up. Your father speaks first.

"The night be with you," he says, making the Sign with his right hand.

"And also with you," your grandfather responds, returning the Sign. His voice is careful, measured, as if he never says anything without thinking.

"I grant you safe passage into my home," your father says. Your parents aren't usually this formal with guests, so he has to pause to remember the words. "May the night deal with me, be it ever so severely, if harm comes to you while under my roof."

Your grandfather nods and walks into the house, taking a seat at the table.

"I was surprised when I did not receive an invitation to Horatius's manhood ceremony," he says.

"We arnaa havin one," your mother says, temporarily lapsing back into the old accent. "We're just having a regular birthday party."

Your grandfather turns his attention to you. "I missed seeing you at our pack's summer festivals."

"We aren't going to take him until he's older," your father says.

"Older?" Your grandfather scoffs. "Does the boy even know who he is?"

Of course you know who you are. You have always known you were Chosen, that you were different than the Others. Every full moon your mother baked a gingerbread man. Your father came home at midnight, symbolizing the conclusion of the hunt, then broke off the head and divided the pieces. Your mother told you in the old country there would be a real hunt, a real Other would be killed and devoured. The Chosen didn't do that anymore, but you still baked the gingerbread man to remember.

"He is Chosen," your grandfather says. He looks down at your plate. "No amount of chocolate birthday cake will change that."

After that day, you see your grandfather more often.

Janus calls you shortly after you get to your mother's house. Your mother doesn't want you to go, is suddenly talkative. She says you just got there, but you issue a quick apology and then you're in her car, which used to be your car, driving farther east.

You meet Janus at a sports bar at the intersection of two large streets that didn't exist when you left El Paso. You worry it might be awkward (you haven't spoken to Janus since you moved to Chicago, even though the two of you used to be best friends). But your fears, at least these ones, are quickly assuaged.

"Horatius my brother!" Janus exclaims as you walk into the bar. He's sitting at a small table with two others. You recognize them both as Chosen but don't remember their names.

There's a jukebox in the corner, but it's just for show. The sound of old 80's power ballads is streaming off the bartender's phone. The music is fighting for attention with the audio from the TVs placed throughout the bar, each showing a different game.

Every seat at every table is occupied. Even the bare areas of the wall are taken up by patrons strategically leaning against them, searching for places to sit. Some simply stand between the tables, shouting to be heard over the music, and the TVs, and other loud conversations.

"The night be with you," you say once you are close enough for Janus to hear you. Janus makes a motion with his hand and the two Chosen get up from the table, leaving two empty seats for you to choose from.

They walk away from the table, towards the bar, and they make the Sign to you as they pass. You're startled at first, not used to seeing the Sign in public, in front of Others, but after a moment of fumbling indecision you free your right hand from your pocket and make the Sign back.

You sit down next to Janus and he hits you on the back, hard.

"The prodigal son has returned," he says. "We were afraid you would never leave Chicago."

"I wouldn't miss the funeral," you say.

"Of course." Janus nods his head solemnly while bowing it slightly. It's like he's a 1950's sitcom dad, like he should have a pipe in his mouth and is about to dispense wisdom to you.

"Your grandfather was a great leader," Janus says. "May he run among the stars."

"May he run among the stars," you repeat.

Janus leans back in his chair. "I'm glad you came Horatius. There are some things I wanted to discuss with you."

"Excuse me, is this seat taken?" The voice belongs to a slim man, mid-20s, standing over the empty chair next to Janus.

"Well, is it?" The man asks again.

Janus turns and looks up at the man. You can't see the look on his face since he's turned from you, but it has some effect on the man because he jumps back a step.

"Okay man, I'll find another chair," he says as he leaves.

Janus turns back to you and smiles. "Now where were we?"

A waitress appears next to Janus and places a plate in front of him.

"Here's your order. Sorry for the wait."

"No problem at all," Janus says, talking to the waitress but never breaking eye contact with you. The waitress leaves, and Janus picks up the item on his plate.

"I wasn't sure when you'd come, so I went ahead and ordered," he says. "I would wait for you to order, but I don't want the food to get cold, and I am absolutely *famished*."

As Janus takes his first bite, eyes still on you, you realize what he's eating. That's why he's looking at you. He wants to see your reaction.

"Are you insane?" you say, looking around. "What are you doing?"

Janus smiles. "Eating dinner," he says. "This place has the best hamburgers in the far east."

You look around again, scared one of the elders is watching, wondering if you'll be punished simply for witnessing this atrocity.

"You're eating meat," you say.

Janus takes another bite. He chews, slowly, and speaks with food still in his mouth.

"I'm not eating *meat*," he says. "I'm eating a double bacon burger with jalapenos, fried onions, and the bar's proprietary spicy sauce." He swallows, thinks for a moment, and moves his burger filled hand towards your face. "Would you like a bite?"

You recoil as if it might bite you. "It's forbidden," you hiss. "You could transform."

"Would that be such a bad thing?"

You start to talk, but Janus makes a motion with his other hand, the one not holding the burger.

"Do you ever think about high school?" he asks.

You shake your head. "I'd rather focus on the present."

"When I think back on our lives, on the summer festivals, on your grandfather, one thing always strikes me." He takes a bite of his hamburger, chews, and swallows. "We were always scared. Everything the elders told us, every story, every exercise, every festival. They said it was all supposed to make us proud of being Chosen, but it wasn't. It was designed to make us scared."

Janus puts down the burger. "What if we weren't scared?"

He looks around the bar at the TVs, the crowded tables, the man who wanted our extra chair. "If I wanted to start a fight right now, I could take out one, maybe two Others, but the crowd would rush me. Heck, there are at least a couple guys in here who could beat me in a one-on-one fight."

Janus lowers his head conspiratorially. "But if I transformed, if we *both* transformed, we could kill every Other in this bar before they knew what hit them."

You start to get up from your chair.

"Where are you going? I'm not finished."

"I am," you say. "This is crazy."

You turn to walk away.

"Horatius, wait."

You stop and turn back to Janus.

"I'm not the only one who feels this way, who thinks we shouldn't live in fear. After your grandfather's funeral, the elders will choose a new Alpha. I'm going to put myself forward for consideration."

"You're only twenty."

"So was your grandfather when he became Alpha. And, it would help my case if the grandson of the previous Alpha would show me his support. Think about it."

"I'll think about it," you say, and then you leave the bar.

You go to your first summer festival a month before you start high school. You are fourteen years old. This is where you meet Janus.

The festival is held west of El Paso, out in the New Mexican desert. For three days and two nights, a large stretch of wilderness is taken over by campers and tents and all manner of grills and cooking fires.

Outside of your family, you've never been in a place where everyone is Chosen. There are almost a hundred Chosen you haven't met before, many your own age. You meet Janus, and the two of you explore the brush, chasing lizards and throwing stones at birds.

On the last day, you meet at a small concrete building, as wide as a two-car garage but only half as tall, at the edge of the campground. You are told it is because you are about to start high school, so it is time for you to undergo the rite.

There are five including you and Janus, and you are ushered into the concrete building by one of the pack elders who is wearing a mask. The ceiling is just barely tall enough for you to stand. You find yourself hunching slightly even though you don't have to. Janus keeps forgetting about the low ceiling, periodically jumping up for fun, even though he scrapes his head in the process.

You all sit down around an upside-down wooden crate. The air inside the room smells old, like fresh bread that has gone stale. You want to get out and go back to the festival.

The other elders walk into the room. They are wearing their formal black robes and black masks over their faces. The masks are carved into fearsome visages that are supposed to show the ferocity of the soul within.

Janus starts to laugh. You turn to him, horrified.

"It's the masks," he says. "They just look so ridiculous."

"Silence!" declares one of the elders. His mask is fiercer than the others, eye slits surrounded by carvings of thorns and razors. You recognize the voice. It's your grandfather.

"What sound does a wolf make?" your grandfather says to those in the room.

Along with the others, you let out a short, "Aahooo."

"What is the call of the Chosen!"

In unison, you all lean your heads back and howl. "AAHOOO!"

Your grandfather walks into the center of the circle, towards the upturned crate, and removes a box from his robe. He opens the box, places it on the crate, and pulls something out.

The room is filled with a new scent, a bitter sweetness, like chocolate being burned. Your grandfather holds up the source of the smell, and you notice he is wearing thick black gloves.

"This is why you are here today," he says to all of you, all the incoming high school freshmen seated around the center crate. "This is what you must learn to fear."

In your grandfather's hand is a green stem with several lavender flowers growing out of it. Each flower is made up of a single hood shaped petal that points downward, as if the flower is too shy to meet your gaze.

The scent, even from that small flower, is overwhelming. You want to leave the room and run out into the open air, but you know you're not supposed to do that.

"This is wolfsbane," your grandfather says. "Remember its scent, remember its shape, remember its color. This flower may be small, but it is deadly to the Chosen. Hold it long enough, and it will seep into your skin and kill you. Smell it long enough, and you will surely die."

"Then why are we smelling it now?" Janus says. He says it sarcastically, like he doesn't believe any of this is real.

"So you'll never forget the smell," your grandfather says. "So you'll run if you ever smell it again."

Burning pain shoots through your body. It's as if a knife has been stabbed between your shoulder blades. You almost collapse, almost scream, but you remember who you are. You are Chosen, you are the grandson of the Alpha, so you show no pain even as the children around you cry and whimper for their mothers.

The pain strikes again, and you realize it's the elders. They are going from child to child, sticking each one with a small black device.

"Remember this pain," your grandfather says. "Remember this pain, and this smell, and if you ever smell it again then let the memory of this pain be your guide. Run."

Your grandfather drops the wolfsbane back into the box and closes it.

"I don't understand," Janus says. It's an hour later, and the two of you are lying in the shade, still smarting from the electric stings. Outside the air is fresh, the slightly dusty smell of air that's traveled across the desert and is resting briefly before it continues its journey.

"If wolfsbane is so dangerous," Janus says. "Why don't we just tell the Others to stop growing it?"

"We can't tell the Others," you say. "Don't you remember the boy who cried wolf?"

Every Chosen child knows the story of the boy who cried wolf. Aeneas was a young Chosen boy back in Italy, back in the old country, whose best friend was an Other named Christopher. Aeneas and Christopher were inseparable, spending their days running through the forest outside their small village and catching tadpoles in a stream.

One hot summer day, the sun beating down so ferociously that even the mosquitos were too tired to bite, Aeneas and Christopher were crossing a small stream when they came face to face with a wolf. Christopher screamed, the wolf snarled, and Christopher went running back to the village, leaving Aeneas behind. When Christopher told the villagers what he had seen, they mounted on fast horses, rifles and swords in hand, and rode into the forest. But instead of a wolf, all they found was Aeneas, sitting by the stream.

The next day, Aeneas and Christopher went to a giant boulder where they would pretend it was a castle and they were its kings. But once again, they saw the wolf. Again, Christopher went running back to the village, leaving Aeneas behind, and told the villagers what he had seen. The villagers mounted on fast horses, rifles and swords in hand. But when they reached the boulder, instead of finding a wolf, all they found was Aeneas sitting at the top, pretending he was king of the castle.

The third day, which was even hotter than the previous two, Aeneas and Christopher went deeper and deeper into the woods until they could no longer see the sun.

Christopher turned to Aeneas. "Why did you not run when you saw the wolf?" he asked. "Were you not scared when it snarled?"

"It wasn't snarling, it was greeting us," Aeneas said. "It wanted to play."

And with that, Aeneas began to transform before Christopher.

"Don't you see Christopher?" Aeneas whispered to his best friend. "I am a wolf too."

Aeneas finished his transformation, and as he did, Christopher screamed. Christopher went running back to the village and told the villagers what he had seen. The villagers mounted on fast horses, rifles and swords in hand, and when they reached the deep forest, when they found Aeneas, they cut off his head and hung it from a tree branch as a warning to all the Chosen of what would happen if they ever revealed themselves.

You and Janus attend the same high school. You take the same bus to school every day, and you are the only two Chosen on the bus. No one else knows you're Chosen of course, but they can sense something is different about the two of you.

"Hey queer, there are a couple empty seats over here. You don't have to sit next to your boyfriend."

The voice is directed at Janus, not at you. They don't bother you, because you just ignore them, but Janus can never resist being baited. The source of the voice is Blaine, a senior not popular enough to have friends who drive cars, who only looks big because you and Janus are still freshmen.

"You talking to me?" Janus says. Janus was scrawny back then. He stands up in the aisle, trying to look angry and fierce, but instead it looks comical, like an infant trying to look mad.

"Yeah, I'm talking to you," Blaine says.

Janus charges him and Blaine, laughing, spins him around into a headlock.

"You like that queer?" Blaine says, still laughing. "You like being held by a real man?"

Janus locks eyes with you, and you can see it. He's trying to transform. He's trying to transform so he can kill Blaine.

You shake your head, and Janus, instead of transforming, begins to cry.

The bus driver keeps driving.

When you go away to college, you see your mother cry for the first and last time.

"Be careful among the Others," she says, ignoring the fact there are just as many Others in El Paso as in Chicago. "Never forget who you are. Never forget you are Chosen."

Chicago smells different than El Paso. It snows in October, not just flurries, but a real snowstorm. You order a slice of pizza, no meat, and eat it while standing on the sidewalk, the icy flakes baptizing you in their coldness. The whole thing reminds you of your father, of driving down a wooded road, except now you have no desire to lean your head back and howl.

You try to eat the pizza with just your hands, but it is Chicago style, thicker than what you're used to. Big clumps of tomato fall onto the sidewalk and onto your hand. You try to lick them off your palm, wondering if this is what it feels like to lick blood off a freshly killed prey.

Cindy has long blonde hair that goes half-way down her back. She wears it with a slight wave, which playfully hides her face behind a curtain of snowy locks, especially when she's reading. You meet Cindy the second week of school, when you and your roommate are playing spades in the dorm common room. She calls you "Ray" because she has trouble pronouncing Horatius. Most of your fellow students call you Ray, and after a while it seems normal. Cindy's never heard of El Paso and asks if it's close to Dallas.

You find out Cindy is in your Introduction to Microeconomics class, so you ask her if she wants to study sometime. On your first date she tells you her favorite film is *Beauty and the Beast*, and if she ever gets married she wants the first dance to be to *Tale as Old as Time*. When you're with Cindy, Chicago feels real and El Paso starts to feel like fantasy.

After your third date she invites you up to her dorm room.

"I've never invited anyone in here before," she says as she opens the door. Her room looks like yours but cleaner, brighter.

And then you smell it, that horrible smell. Your gaze is yanked toward a small box on the dresser, right by Cindy's bed. As you feel electric shocks stabbing into your back over and over, Cindy sees where you're looking.

"I know, it smells a little weird, doesn't it," she confesses. "It's this flower called wolfsbane. My grandmother gave it to me before I left for college. She's from Italy, and she believes young unmarried women have to keep wolfsbane by their bed, or in the middle of the night werewolves will come and bite them. Crazy, right?"

You grimace, and you make an excuse to leave, but you call Cindy again the next day.

The elders begin the meeting just after sundown. Your grandfather's funeral earlier that day was a spectacle, but this is the real event. The elders, along with the other important members of the pack, meet out in the New Mexican desert, in the same place where they hold the summer festival.

There is a great bonfire in the center and two flaming torches on either side of the space where the elders are standing. The rest of the pack stands or sits on the rocky ground around them.

Your mother is there, as the representative of your family. Janus stands next to her, and when he sees you arrive he makes an excuse to walk over.

"I'm glad you came over to my side," he says.

One of the elders, the one leading the ceremony, is starting to speak, so Janus runs back to his place. You tune out the first part of the speech, but your ears perk up when you hear the elder ask, "Does anyone come to support Janus's bid to lead us?"

You step forward and Janus smiles.

You look around at all those gathered. "I come forward to challenge Janus's bid to lead us."

Janus looks stunned. "What are you doing?" he hisses. You ignore him.

The elder speaking, like the others, is wearing his traditional black mask. You can't see his face, but his voice sounds confused. "There are no challenges, little one. The elders vote on the candidates for leadership."

"I don't want a vote," you say. You thought you would be more nervous, but you're on auto-pilot now, doing what needs to be done. "I want a challenge, a decision by combat. The winner becomes the new Alpha."

There is silence among those gathered. The fire flickers, sending bitter smoke up into the air. Even the wildlife is quiet, content to leave this sacred gathering alone.

You look at the pack assembled around you.

"What sound does a wolf make!" you yell.

There is no reply.

You plant your feet and scream out, "What's the call of the Chosen!"

There is silence again. But then you hear it. A single howl.

"Aahooo!"

Then it is joined by others, and others.

"AAHOOO! AAHOOO!"

Soon, well over half the pack is howling. They can't help it, the response is ingrained in their very souls.

You turn to the elder.

"It's the old way," you say. "It's what my grandfather would have wanted."

This seems to satisfy the elder, who nods his head.

"Janus, do you accept this challenge?"

You've been avoiding looking at Janus, but now that you do, you can see Janus has murder in his eyes. They look just like they did that time on the bus, but this time you are the source of their rage.

"I accept this challenge," he says.

"Very well," says the elder. "Then before the challenge begins, let us pray."

As one, the elders bow their heads. Janus does too. You see your chance.

When the elders start to pray, you rip Janus's throat out with your teeth. You cross the space between the two of you in three quick steps and grab hold of his shoulders with your hands. Your speed and ferocity surprises even you. Janus doesn't have time to transform, just to stand there in shock. You've never done this before, but it seems so natural. You open your mouth as wide as it can go, fasten your jaw around Janus's jugular (this all happens in under a second) and bite down as hard as you can. The taste is slightly rubbery, then your teeth bite through as Janus opens his mouth to scream. You motion downward with your head and the entire throat rips off of his body and onto the ground.

Blood sprays out of Janus's carotid artery. The taste of so much blood makes you heady, like fumes from paint. You step back, spitting the blood from your mouth, as Janus's body collapses to the ground. His body spasms once. Then, stillness.

You look around at the elders. At first you thought they might try to intervene, but now you can see their approval, see they were just as afraid as you were of what Janus would do as Alpha. You can see Janus's friends, the ones from the bar as well as others, standing off to the side. They want to kill you, but you have the elders' blessing now, so they won't touch you. The pack is safe, at least for now.

In the morning you'll go back to Chicago, to Cindy, and you'll tell her what you are. Maybe she'll accept it, and you'll live happily ever after in Chicago. Maybe she'll reject you, and you'll return to El Paso to lead the pack just as your grandfather did. You don't know what the future will hold, but you are at peace, because your surroundings don't change who you are, and you know who you are.

You are Chosen.

Killing Mister Oni

The vase hit the floor with a crash. Every item of furniture in the living room shuddered at the impact. Shards of broken ceramic scattered across the imitation wood laminate and under couches and tables.

Mom came running into the living room, apron askew and hands coated in flour.

"David, what did you do?"

From my vantage point huddled on the couch, knees pulled to my chest, I sniffed and shook my head.

"It wasn't me Mom. It was Mister Oni!"

Mom sighed, brushed her hands against her apron, and looked sternly into the corner of the living room where the remains of the vase lay.

"Mister Oni, you are in big trouble."

I shook my head. "He's not there mom, he's over there." I pointed at the adjacent corner, where the tall turquoise floor lamp stood watch over the living room. The sound of the breaking vase had startled Mister Oni, and now he kept running laps around the lamp, his top hat knocked askew and his monocle holding on for dear life.

"What in the world is that racket?"

Dad emerged from his study. His tie was loosened, his shirt cuffs were unbuttoned, and his face was red.

Mom crossed her arms.

"Your son's familiar broke my limited edition Acoma Pueblo vase."

"He didn't mean to!"

Dad's eyes locked on me. "Are you crying David?"

I shook my head and sniffed. "No."

Dad rubbed his temple. "This is great, just great. Jeffrey has been riding me all week about our presentation to headquarters next month, the garage door is broken, again, and now your giant guinea pig is breaking vases."

"He's not a guinea pig Dad, he's a capybara!"

Mister Oni had finally tired of running. Panting just a little, he trotted up next to where I was seated on the couch. I readjusted Mister Oni's top hat, then he jumped up next to me. I stroked his back, calming him so he would stop shaking.

"This is ridiculous," Dad said. "The boy is too old to still have a familiar."

Mom turned to go back into the kitchen. "He turns ten in two days. The Law says he has until then to get rid of it."

Dad exhaled. "Well until then young man, you have to clean up after him." With a huff, Dad turned and went back into his study.

Mister Oni looked up at me. He had finally stopped shaking. His snout was a little wet, and there was a tear in his right eye, behind his monocle.

"I'm sorry, David," he said in his usual slow southern drawl.

"It's okay, Mister Oni. I know you didn't mean to."

Mister Oni looked at the broken vase.

"Do you want me to help clean up, David?"

I shook my head. "I got it."

Mister Oni blinked. "Are we still best friends, David?"

I smiled. "The best."

Mom made meatloaf for dinner, with a mixture of steamed peas and carrots on the side. I managed to separate the carrots from the peas while Mom and Dad weren't looking, then palm them into my hand and pass them to Mister Oni where he sat next to my feet under the table.

"I killed my familiar with my bare hands when I was only eight years old," Dad said. He was on his third glass of wine already, even though it was still dinnertime, and he had told this story before. "I squeezed his neck with my two hands and screamed at him that I was a big boy and didn't need a familiar anymore. I squeezed him until he stopped flailing, stopped twitching, and then I threw his body on the ground."

Dad slammed his wine glass down onto the table.

"Now David, just because your father strangled his familiar with his bare hands, that doesn't mean you have to as well," Mom said. "A month before my tenth birthday, I simply told my familiar it was time for her to go away, and she did. That's what most people do."

Dad snorted. "Sure Mary, that's a fine solution. If you expect the rest of your problems in life to just… walk away when you tell them to."

Mister Oni kept eating his carrots. He munched loudly, pretending he couldn't hear the conversation. But I knew he could.

Mom looked at me. "Tomorrow is your last day as a nine year old, David, so you're going to have to let Mister Oni go."

"He would kill him if he were a real man," Dad mumbled.

Mister Oni kept munching.

"I know it's hard, David," Mom continued. "But it has to be done. It's not just what the Law says, it's the way things work. Your familiar is supposed to help you grow up, but when you turn ten, you need to start growing on your own. Be more independent and all that. If your familiar sticks around, then you can never truly grow up. And you don't want that, do you?"

I shook my head. "Of course, not Mom."

"Then be a man and kill the thing," Dad said.

The four of us kept eating.

When it was time to go to bed, I dove under my blanket while Mom stood at the door to my bedroom. Mister Oni dutifully trotted into the room and lay down on his spot inside the closet. I made sure the blanket completely covered my feet before nodding to Mom. She turned off the lights and closed the door.

I lay there in the dark. There was some light from my window, but not enough to provide comfort. Instead the light cast a spiderweb of shadows across the room. The blanket was warm, and I was getting hot. But I couldn't move. I had to stay absolutely still. If I didn't move, maybe I would be safe.

I tried to match each shadow with the object that generated it. That one shadow creeping up the ceiling towards me was just my soccer trophy from last year. The shadow lurking in the corner was just a lamp. But there was a large shadow against the bedroom door. As much as I tried, I couldn't find its source. It looked like it was moving, getting bigger.

"Mister Oni!" I tried to whisper, but instead almost yelled it.

There was a rustle, followed by the sound of pattering feet. I heard

Mister Oni approach the bed, then felt the impact as he jumped onto it. Mister Oni snuggled up next to me.

"Is everything okay, David?" he asked in his slow southern drawl.

I nodded my head. I could move my body again. The shadows forgotten, I felt sleep starting to call.

"Once you're gone, I don't think I'll ever be able to go to sleep," I said. "I'll have to leave the lights on all the time."

"You'll find a way, David. You'll be ten soon. That's all grown up."

"I don't want to be grown up. Not if it means you have to go away."

Mister Oni settled into the blanket, his top hat resting against the pillow.

"I'm here for now, David. Nothing to fear as long as I'm here."

With that, I drifted off to sleep.

I decided to do it when I got home from school. Even though my legs were relatively short, Mister Oni had to run to keep up with me whenever I walked. Usually on the walk home from school we talked about whether we would use that day's screen time to play *Myst* or watch *X-Men*, or who we would try to get back at someday for making fun of us at school.

This time we were both quiet. When we got to my driveway, I looked down at Mister Oni. He looked up at me, his top hat perfectly straight and his monocle properly adjusted.

"Mister Oni, I think it's time for you to leave."

Mister Oni stood there.

"I mean it Mister Oni." I tucked my thumbs under the straps of my backpack. "Tomorrow I turn ten, so this is the last day I'm allowed to have a familiar. So leave. Go away."

The reflection of the sun gave a sheen to Mister Oni's coat of fur. Mister Oni yawned, exposing the large white teeth at the front of his mouth.

This wasn't working. It was supposed to work!

"Why aren't you leaving?"

Mister Oni blinked his eyes, the monocle managing to stay in place. "Do you want me to leave?"

"Of course I want you to leave. I turn ten tomorrow, you have to go. That's the Law."

"But do *you* want me to leave?"

I sat down on the sidewalk and sighed. "No. No, I don't want you to leave."

Mister Oni snuggled against my leg.

"Then I can't leave, David," Mister Oni drawled. "I'm your familiar, I do what you want. And if you don't really want me to leave, then I can't leave, even if you tell me to."

I reached out and stroked Mister Oni's back.

"But what if I get in trouble? What if my parents find out? Or the Law does?"

Mister Oni purred. "It'll be okay, David. Nothing to fear as long as I'm here."

My alarm clock woke me. It blared the *Transformers* theme song until I hit the large red button that turned it off. Mister Oni wasn't lying next to me like he usually was, like he had every day for as long as I could remember.

My stomach turned. I was ten now. Mister Oni was gone, that's all there was to it. I sat up, looking around just in case. I didn't have to look for long.

Mister Oni was standing on the floor next to my bed, staring at me. He had to have woken up earlier, before the alarm. His eyes were slightly red, as if he hadn't slept much the night before, and his fur looked slightly tussled.

"Mister Oni, you're still here." I said it softly, in case my parents were listening.

"Of course, David. I'll be here as long as you need me."

I smiled. "Until I can go to sleep by myself in the dark."

Mister Oni smiled back. "Until you're all grown up."

Mom made banana chocolate chip pancakes for breakfast.

"Happy Birthday, sweetie!" she said.

"Happy Birthday," Dad mumbled from behind his newspaper.

I sat down in my chair. Mister Oni took up his usual post underneath the table, next to my feet.

Mom put a plate of pancakes down in front of me.

"How did you sleep last night?" Mom asked. "Was it hard without Mister Oni?"

Dad grunted behind his newspaper. "Stupid giant guinea pig."

"He's a… he was a capybara, Dad, not a guinea pig."

Dad grunted again.

Mom sat down at her seat and poured syrup on her own pancakes. "Well your father and I are very proud of you for sending Mister Oni away. It's a sign you're really growing up."

I smiled. "You guys taught me how."

Making sure my parents weren't looking, I broke off a piece of pancake and handed it to Mister Oni under the table. I smiled at my parents again as Mister Oni happily munched away.

When I got to school, Suzy ran up to greet me.

"Happy Birthday, David!" She handed me a card made out of red construction paper. "I made it myself."

"Thank you," I said. Mister Oni gave a snort of contempt. He had walked slower than usual on the way to school, and he was wheezing just a little.

"Big whoop, you're still a kid." It was Andrew. Andrew had to do first grade twice, so he was already eleven.

Suzy ignored him. "Was it hard sending Mister Oni away?"

I shrugged. "I just told him to go. It was no big deal."

"I remember when I sent my familiar away," Suzy said. "I cried for a whole week."

"I'm sure David already cried this morning," Andrew said. He pushed me on the shoulder. "Isn't that right David? Are we going to see some more tears later today?"

"Don't push him." It was Mister Oni. The others couldn't hear him of course, but I could.

I looked down. "It's okay. Andrew's just trying to be funny."

Mister Oni growled.

Suzy's eyes narrowed. "Who are you talking to?"

Mister Oni's growl grew louder. His white teeth were just a little yellow, and his eyes looked even redder than before.

Andrew's eyes opened wide. "Wait a minute, you're talking to your familiar. He's still here, isn't he!"

With a final growl, Mister Oni launched himself at Andrew's right leg. Andrew screamed. Mister Oni's giant teeth bit through Andrew's jeans and sank into his soft flesh. Andrew collapsed to the ground.

"Get him off me!" Andrew screamed.

"Mister Oni, stop it!"

I grabbed Mister Oni, who was holding firmly to Andrew's leg like a dog with a chew toy. Dark blood leaked out of Andrew's jeans where Mister Oni's teeth were fixed to his leg. With all my strength, I pulled

Mister Oni away and we both fell to the ground. There was a crack down the center of Mister Oni's monocle. His top hat had a dent in it towards the top.

Andrew stared, his eyes full of fear. "You still have your familiar. You're ten today, and you still have your familiar. I'm going to tell a teacher!"

Suzy looked at me with horror. "What were you thinking David? You can't still have a familiar. The Law forbids it!"

I turned and ran. Mister Oni ran after me, sprinting as fast as his little legs would carry him. When we got to my house Dad was already gone at work. It was Wednesday, which meant Mom would be at the mall most of the day, so I waited at the side of the house until I saw Mom's car pull out and drive away.

I used the spare key under the mat to get into the house. I paced back and forth in the living room as Mister Oni sat on the couch.

"What are we going to do?"

Mister Oni blinked his eyes as he looked up at me. "Are you mad, David?"

"Of course I'm mad. You bit Andrew, and now everyone is going to know I didn't get rid of you yesterday when I was still nine, when I was supposed to."

Mister Oni looked down, the dent in his top hat staring up at me. "I'm sorry, David. But I don't like it when people make fun of you." He lifted his snout and looked at me, red lines crisscrossing the whites of his eyes. "People who make fun of you need to pay the price."

"What are we going to do?" I put my hand on Mister Oni's back to pet him, and he felt warmer than usual. "The school is going to call my parents, or the Law, and then they'll make you leave."

"I have an idea, David," Mister Oni said. "But first I need to know, are we still best friends?"

I swallowed. "We'll always be best friends."

"And you'd do anything to keep it that way?" Mister Oni's gaze looked through my eyes and into my soul.

"Mister Oni, you're scaring me."

Mister Oni stared at me silently, his body still. He did it so long I would have thought him dead if it hadn't been for his labored breathing.

"We can go to the Cave," he said at last.

I sniffled. "The Cave? But it's so dark. I can't go in there."

Mister Oni's eyes watered. "Don't you see, David? You need me. You can't live without me. And the Cave is the one place where we can be safe. Forever."

I gulped.

"But first, David, there's something I need you to do. Something I need you to get for me, to bring with you to the cave."

Even though there was no one else in the house, Mister Oni whispered what I was supposed to do next.

Dad's study was off-limits. I had never been inside, though I had looked in from the hallway on occasion. When I opened the door, I thought blaring alarms and flashing lasers would go off. Instead, there was nothing. The furniture and papers sat where they always did, paying me no attention as I entered the forbidden realm.

I walked behind Dad's large mahogany desk and opened the bottom right drawer, the one Mister Oni told me to look in. It swung open to reveal a small gray safe.

"Try his birthday," Mister Oni had told me. It was as if I could hear Mister Oni's voice with me in the study as I turned the four dials. "Zero Four One Nine. It'll work, David. Trust me."

When the fourth dial was in place, I tugged on the safe door. It opened. Inside was a black pistol, just like the ones on TV.

"Don't forget the magazines too," Mister Oni had told me. "The gun won't work without them."

There were two magazines in the safe. I put one of them inside the gun, the way the police do in the movies, and put the other one in my pocket. I was ready to go.

My neighborhood sat at the edge of the city's suburban sprawl. Behind the neighborhood, hidden in a series of small hills, was the Cave. No one knew who first discovered the Cave, but it was a legend at my school. When walking through the hills, the Cave looked like a ditch in the ground. But once you jumped down and stood in the ditch, you could see a small crevice at the edge of the bottom. The crevice was the entrance to a tunnel which burrowed into the hill before ending in a large cavern. The tunnel was long and narrow enough that the interior of the cavern was pitch black. Or so I had been told. I had visited the Cave's entrance, but never gone inside.

Andrew went inside once. He did it over summer vacation, and when school started again he bragged to everyone at recess about how brave he had been. He also confirmed the rumors that there were all manner of ghosts and monsters inside the Cave. Suzy said he was just making it up, but something about the way he described it made me think he was telling the truth.

I arrived at the Cave just as the sun was starting to set. When I jumped down into the ditch, as I had done before, it was darker than the ground above. The walls of the ditch blocked the sun's rays, stopping them from illuminating the tunnel that guarded the Cave's entrance.

I pulled a small flashlight out of my pocket, one Mom gave to me last year for my birthday. I took the pistol out of my other pocket. I got down on my knees, lowering my head to the bottom of the ditch until the crevice was just in front of my face.

"Mister Oni, are you in there?" I called into the tunnel.

No answer.

I shined my flashlight into the crevice. I could see the first foot of the tunnel, but no more. Even with the flashlight, it was so dark.

I didn't have to go into that darkness. I could leave. I could run back home and tell the Law that I had sent Mister Oni away. No one would ever know.

But I would know. And Mister Oni would still be there in the Cave, waiting. He had already bit Andrew, who knew what else he would do? Who else he would hurt.

I shook my head. He was my familiar. I had to handle it.

Shuffling my legs, I lay down at the bottom of the ditch. With the flashlight in one hand and the pistol in the other, I used my legs to push my body, head first, into the tunnel.

With one push of the legs, my body was halfway in. It was tight, even tighter than it looked. I pushed more with my legs, but it wasn't enough to move me. I reached out and placed the flashlight and pistol a few feet in front of my face, then used the tips of my fingers to pull myself farther in. It worked. I moved, just a little.

I repeated the action. I tossed the flashlight and pistol in front of me, then pulled myself even with them. The flashlight lit up a piece of the tunnel in front of me, but not all of it. I felt rocks around me on all sides. I imagined how much rock there was right on top of me, threatening to come down.

"Mister Oni!" I called out.

"I'm right here, David." The voice was distant, and the distance gave it a strange echo. "Just keep on coming."

Toss. Pull. Toss. Pull. After an eternity, I felt a larger empty space in front of me. With a final push, I emerged into the cavern. It was bigger than I expected, bigger even than Andrew's description. The weak beam of light revealed magnificent stalactites, shadowy ceilings, and murky gray walls.

But as I stood up, the flashlight clattered to the floor. The collision with the ground turned it off.

Darkness surrounded me. Darker than my bedroom at night, darker than the scary rides at amusement parks. Pure darkness.

"Mister Oni?"

"I'm right here, David."

The voice came from every direction at once. I looked around, trying to find the source of the voice, but all I saw was darkness. I dropped to my knees, feeling for the flashlight. My left hand found only rock. My right hand held tight to the pistol.

"Did you bring what I asked for, David?"

"Where are you Mister Oni?"

Still nothing, just rough rock. No flashlight.

"I'm right here. Where's the gun, David?"

I kept searching. "Why won't you tell me where you are, Mister Oni?"

"I already told you, David."

My left hand felt the smooth plastic of the flashlight. I whipped it up and turned it on, illuminating the capybara two feet in front of me.

Mister Oni grinned. "I'm right here."

His top hat was ripped in two. His teeth were pure yellow. Fluid leaked out of his red eyes. His coat was matted with sweat.

"Now we can be together forever, David."

I raised the pistol and pulled the trigger. The pistol leapt in my hand, an instant of fire and smoke filling the cavern like a camera flash. Mister Oni fell back, out of the range of my flashlight.

I moved the flashlight around until I captured Mister Oni again. He was against the wall of the cavern, panting as red liquid seeped into his fur.

"You're not afraid of the dark anymore, David," he said.

A tear fell out of my eye and onto my cheek. "You taught me how."

Mister Oni smiled. "Nothing to fear as long as I'm here."

I pulled the trigger again, and again, and again, and I didn't stop until Mister Oni's body stopped twitching. Then I dropped the pistol, turned around, and crawled out of the Cave.

180

My perfect moment? Well, the story starts many years ago, back before the Freeze, just after I returned from the war. This was before I married Mara, before I even knew her. I needed a place to live, so I moved into a second-floor studio at the Pasado Lane Apartments on the east side, right off Montana and George Dieter. Apartment 180.

Here's what I remember. My eyes snapped open as the cheap digital alarm clock turned from 1:59 to 2:00. A blanket lay in a heap on the floor. My surroundings came into focus. I was lying on the couch. Home. Safe. Yet I had woken up at two in the morning, just as I had every morning since I returned from overseas.

My feet swung down onto the shag carpet. The thud of my heartbeats drowned out the couple arguing downstairs and the drunk singing to himself somewhere down the street. I sat there for a moment, willing my heart to beat softer, slower. No use.

Standing up, I made my way through the interior of the apartment, my own private kingdom. The brown leather couch I slept on sat peacefully behind a Walmart coffee table I used as both desk and dining room. Ten DVDs stood at attention below the TV stand. The artificial vanilla scent of my air freshener drifted over from the kitchen counter.

Apartment 180 had a tiny porch overlooking the parking lot, illuminated by a single bare light bulb. An upside-down plastic crate sat next to a metal folding chair the previous tenant forgot in the closet.

I sat in the chair and looked out over the parking lot. The midsummer night breeze felt chilly, but not cold. The air smelled like creosote. The clouds above me looked overly ripe, as if they had engorged themselves on water and now could barely hold it in. The pack of cigarettes from the previous night watched me from its perch atop the upside-down plastic crate.

The air around me felt tangible, like a tight t-shirt slowly suffocating me. I had no idea what the future held. I had no idea what I was going to do now. I lit a cigarette, drew in a deep breath, and exhaled.

That's when it started to rain. It happened all at once without warning, an explosion of water from the sky. I sat on my metal folding chair, on my tiny balcony, while outside the fountains of heaven poured out onto the earth, blessing the ground and washing away everyone's sins.

And as I inhaled another lungful of smoke and breathed out into the rain-soaked air, sitting there on the balcony of Apartment 180, my heart stopped beating so loudly. My soaring thoughts landed calmly on the ground. Somehow, as I watched the rain, I knew that everything was going to be okay.

Years later I decided to return to Apartment 180 to recreate that moment. It was a Tuesday morning, two months after the Freeze. I made the decision Monday night, but decided to wait until morning to set out on my journey. I needed a good night's sleep.

Mara hated alarms. After we got married, she pleaded with me to let the sun's rays wake us up each morning. She said it was more natural. But after the Freeze, I had to use the alarm on my watch. For obvious reasons, I could no longer depend on the sun to rouse me from my nightly slumber. The clocks in the house, like all clocks everywhere, were frozen at 8:02pm, but my watch, and its alarm, kept time as long as I had it on my wrist. Those were the rules after all.

That morning my watch's alarm pulled me from my dreams at six a.m. on the dot. I rolled off the living room couch and turned off the alarm, silencing its endless squawk. The couch wasn't as comfortable as the bed, but I hadn't slept in my bed since the Freeze. I prepared for my journey.

My gear took up the entire surface of the dining room table Mara's parents gave us for our fifth anniversary. There was my old ruck sack from the Army, the one with the discontinued camouflage pattern that never did blend into anything. A sleeping bag, the light one, and a rolled-up pad to put it on. A box of granola bars, just in case I had trouble foraging. Three pairs of extra socks and underwear. A camelback, already full of water. A small redlight flashlight, in case I needed to see something in the dark without giving away my location. My M4, disassembled, cleaned, and reassembled the night before. And ammo – lots of ammo.

It would only take a couple minutes to throw everything into the ruck. I had time to tell Mara goodbye.

Mara was upstairs, curled into a fetal position on our bed in the master bedroom. Her face was buried in a pillow, hidden under a halo of shoulder length amber hair.

I stood beside the bed, looking down at her frozen form. I reached out a hand but pulled it back before it could touch her.

"Hey, hon, it's me. I'm going to go on a trip, and I wanted to let you know so you wouldn't worry."

No response.

"I'll lock the door behind me so you'll be safe. Even if someone breaks in, they probably won't come up to the bedroom. I mean, when I break into houses, I always leave the bedrooms alone."

Mara remained silent and unmoving. Just as she had since the Freeze.

"Anyways, I'll see you soon. Love you. Goodbye."

Outside it was dark, like it always was now. A full moon peaked over the desert to the north, frozen just like everything else at 8:02pm. The streetlights were on, but they didn't flicker. You don't notice how much streetlights flicker until they don't. Without the flicker the light is too steady and even. It looks unnatural. Not to mention the various flies and mosquitoes caught in the light's beam, frozen forever in their quest to find the light's source.

Around the corner from our house was the neighborhood's communal mailbox. Mrs. O'Neil stood next to her slot, right index finger stuck halfway up her nose.

"Good morning, Mrs. O'Neill," I said as I walked by. I knew she wouldn't respond, but I still did it out of habit. Bet she wouldn't have picked her nose if she knew she'd be stuck like that for all time.

A few houses down, Patricia watered the red oleander in her front yard. A majestic arch of water connected the hose in her hand to the bush on the other end. I almost touched the water with my hand, just to see how it would feel, but I resisted the temptation.

The next house had an aroma of grilled steaks wafting onto the street from the backyard. I remembered those steaks. The first week after the Freeze, I took an inventory of the food in the neighborhood. The steaks were one of the first things I ate. I worried they would go bad. That was back before I understood the rules.

Nothing changes, nothing gets old or goes bad, unless you touch it. Then it starts to move again, like the watch on my wrist.

Of course, that rule doesn't hold true for living things, like people. People like Mara. For people who are frozen, nothing, not even touch, can bring them back.

As I walked, I kept my feet close to the road, lifting them only as high as necessary in a shuffle like motion. It still sounded loud in the absence of any other sound, but I figured I'd be safe. Usually the Mad Ones didn't come this far west.

My path meandered through various neighborhoods, always following a generally southern direction. I took Westwind until it connected to Mesa. There were entire stretches of road with no cars or people, the legacy of the many who had already been home when the Freeze took place. But then I'd walk by a house with a wide-open window, lights on inside, the shadow of one of the frozen staring out into the road. I'd drop my eyes to avoid making eye contact with someone who could not, would never, be able to look back at me.

After ten hours on the road, I took refuge in a tiny blue one-story house close to downtown. I had to try five in a row before I found one that was unlocked. Sure you can kick down a door, but then everyone for miles will hear you and know where you are. The interior lights were off, but enough light came from the streetlights outside, through the open shutters, to make out a maze of moving boxes strewn throughout the compact living room.

No bodies in the room, that was good. The thought of spending a night in someone else's house was unnerving enough without having to look at that person while I did it. On a dining room table covered with crumpled newspapers sat a plate with two slices of pepperoni pizza. My eyes flicked towards the hallway, which led to two closed doors. The pizza's owner would be somewhere back there.

The moment I sat on the couch, still wrapped tightly in plastic sheeting, I felt the fatigue flow down through my body and out my feet. The plastic didn't matter, the couch underneath was so soft that my entire body melted into it. The pizza was still warm, just as it had been when the house's occupant took it out of a box somewhere in the kitchen. In the silence of the house, the sound of my jaw chewing shouted like a jackhammer, but it didn't matter. I was inside the house, and its walls were thick enough to conceal my actions.

There was a knock on the door. I froze. Maybe I imagined it. The knock came again. With my left hand I put the pizza down on the couch while with my right I grabbed my M4. I switched the selector from safe to semi.

"Is there anyone in there?" The voice was female.

I stood, cringing at the plastic squeak that filled the whole room. With one motion I yanked open the door. Staring up at me was a middle-aged woman, at least half a foot shorter than me. Her black hair, a messy tangle of curls, half obscured her face. Her eyes looked tired, unsteady, like they were looking through me instead of at me.

"Good evening, sir," she said. "I'm very sorry to bother you, but have you seen any babies?"

I did a quick scan behind the woman. The street had a half dozen cars in the middle of it, frozen on their way to wherever they had been going, but there were no people. Maybe it wasn't a trap.

I lowered the M4 and nodded towards the couch. "Why don't you come in? It's safer inside."

"Thank you, you're so kind." The woman walked past me.

I laid the M4 on the floor as the woman sat down on the couch, sending another shrill squeak into the world. The door was closed though. No one outside could have heard that.

"Why did you ask me about babies?"

The woman reclined back into the couch. She looked just as relaxed as I had a moment ago. Her eyes closed.

"Did you notice how everything is different now?" she asked. "How no one is moving?"

I nodded, even though her eyes were closed.

"I was working at labor and delivery when it happened. I'm a nurse you see. One moment everyone is running around like puppies chasing a chew toy. Then there was that awful sound, and poof, everyone stops moving. It was quiet, you can't imagine, so quiet. To tell you the truth I was almost relieved. Sure, I knew something was wrong, but it was so peaceful.

"But then I heard it. A baby. It was soft at first, just a whimper. Then it grew louder, a full-on cry. All the babies I could see had frozen in place, just like the adults. And yet, I could hear one crying. I went from room to room, floor to floor, trying to find her, but... but I just couldn't."

The nurse looked up at me. "How many of us do you think there are? That weren't frozen?"

I shrugged. "Not many. About one in a thousand I figure."

The nurse nodded. "That means in our city there are what, seven hundred, eight hundred people still moving around? For the adults it's easy enough to find food. But what about the babies? What about the children? What if there's some two-month-old out there whose entire family is frozen, and now she's just lying there, crying in a crib, no one around to hear her?"

The nurse sniffled.

I cleared my throat. "Listen, what you're doing sounds noble and all, but," I waved my hand at the world around us. "It's been over two months since the Freeze. If there was some helpless baby out there, it's dead."

The nurse shook her head violently. "No, no that can't be. Because, because I can still hear her." She drew in closer to me and her voice became a frantic whisper. "The baby from the hospital. I can still hear her crying."

The only thing I could hear was my heart beating in my chest. Wait, that wasn't my heart. The noise was coming from outside the house. It was a slow, rhythmic thud. Drums. The nurse's eyes opened wide, as did mine.

"Mad Ones," she whispered.

My eyes darted from one corner of the room to another, searching for any sign of occupancy visible from the outside. The door was shut. Unlocked, but you couldn't tell that from outside. The lights were all off. The shutters were open, giving a view of the street, but it was brighter outside than inside so they shouldn't be able to see us. Just in case, the nurse and I both crouched on the ground, eyes peering over the couch at the coming menace.

The Mad Ones crept over the road like a slow tide coming onto shore. The front line of their advance ebbed and flowed. There were dozens of them. They crouched low to the ground as they walked, like feral beings from a lunatic's night terror. Instead of simply walking around obstacles, they darted around them, sometimes jumping on the hood of a car and sometimes crawling underneath it, no rhyme or reason to their twisted dance.

Their leader, Malachi, paraded shirtless at the front of their ranks. A wild beard covered the lower half of his face. The pale moonlight reflected off his bare pasty chest, so white he looked like a corpse. He marched in an exaggerated fashion, each knee grasping up towards the heavens before the attached foot crashed into the depths below. Meanwhile, in perfect time, the drum continued its inexorable beat.

Without warning, Malachi screamed. The scream had no discernable words, just raw rage. An uninhibited bellow of tires screeching and nails dragging down chalkboards and wounded animals crying for their mothers.

The drum ceased mid-beat. The Mad Ones froze in place. As one, they turned their heads towards their leader.

Malachi, eyes wide open, pointed a single bony finger towards a car resting a dozen yards in front of him. The eyes darted to the vehicle.

Then, they were all screaming. The Mad Ones were running, a tsunami instead of a tide. They fell on the car, bashing it with bats, crowbars, even their own arms and legs. The occupant of the car, an elderly man frozen in the act of obeying a stop sign, was pulled from the vehicle and thrown to the ground.

It might have been my imagination, but I could smell the blood as the Mad Ones ripped his body open, scattering parts all over the street. Next to me, the nurse gagged.

No one knew how the Mad Ones chose the targets they did. They roamed throughout the city, walking past some stores, homes, and churches, then randomly meting out destruction to others. They attacked with animalistic fury, purging vestiges of the old world with their rage.

Those few of us who remained unfrozen reacted differently to the Freeze. Some kept going to work, putting on a suit and tie each day and driving to the office until their cars ran out of gas. Apparently others went door to door looking for helpless babies. And the Mad Ones? They just destroyed.

I didn't set an alarm. I stayed awake at least an hour after the Mad Ones departed, but I still worried an alarm, any noise at all, might draw them to me. The nurse continued on her journey, knocking on doors, chasing the source of the crying she insisted she heard, and I continued on mine.

My path took me through downtown. I passed a homeless man holding out an empty worn out Starbucks cup, his eyes looking forlornly ahead. Crying out for help, now for all eternity.

Overhead, office buildings looked up at the sky, waiting to see if the moon would ever stray from its final resting place. Lit-up office windows looked like little eyes. The buildings were frozen giants with a thousand eyes.

Through some windows I saw the silhouettes of worker drones sitting behind their desks, typing away for eternity. Still in the office at 8:02pm. They probably planned to go home early, catch a TV show, go to bed. But instead they wanted to format one last spreadsheet, knock out one last email. Now they were stuck at their desks forever.

From downtown I took Montana Avenue going east. Montana was busier than Mesa had been. I stuck to the middle of the road, dodging around the cars stopped in place. I didn't like walking on the sidewalks. Sure, there were fewer people on the sidewalks than cars on the street, but cars were easy to walk around. Each time I came across a person though, I had to keep them at a far distance. It wasn't like the frozen people in my neighborhood. These were strangers.

I was sore from the day before, but the journey had become easier. I sang songs in my head and sometimes imagined it was the time before the Freeze, and I was out for a stroll.

I approached the intersection where Montana and Paisano merge. I used to hate this intersection, detested trying to look over my shoulder to see whether a car was about to hit me. But now it was still, silent, peaceful.

Out of habit, I spared a quick look over my shoulder as I went through the intersection to see if anyone else was coming.

Scattered across the street were the Mad Ones. They were so still they looked frozen. But there was no mistaking what they were. My feed skidded to a halt. Fifty, sixty sets of eyes flickered in my direction. I gripped my M4 tighter, switching the selector from safe to semi. I was out in the open. There was nowhere to run.

Like marble statues coming to life, the Mad Ones began to move. Their muscles flexed and their heads titled. They moved their limbs experimentally this way and that. Those that had been standing tall crouched down, ready to pounce.

At their lead, Malachi remained a statue, eyes focused directly ahead. Towards me.

I relaxed my grasp on the M4 and gingerly placed it on the cold hard asphalt. There were too many of them, and they were too close. There was no way I could get them all. I put down my ruck sack as well, letting it fall to the ground with a thump.

The drummer behind Malachi began his mournful staccato.

With the eyes of the Mad Ones upon me, I walked towards Malachi. From close up, his beard looked like a living creature reaching out from his chin to entrap the world around it. His eyes were a window to a fire within his soul. The fire's intensity spilled out into the world around him, striving to set it on fire as well.

Malachi maintained his focus on me as I approached. The drum beat louder. A foot away from him, so close we were almost touching, I stopped.

The drum ceased. As if on cue, Malachi screamed. It was the same unearthly scream I heard before at the house with the nurse, and countless other times alone in my home when the sound of his cries of terror carried across the emptiness of the city.

I planted my feet firmly on the ground. I maintained eye contact as best as I could. Then, I screamed too. I screamed about neighbors frozen in the act of fighting, and women picking their nose while getting the mail, and steak I couldn't eat anymore because it was all gone even though the smell still lingered. I screamed about starving crying babies all alone in a frozen world, and the sun that never rose and the moon that never set. And as I screamed, as my skin grew so warm I felt like I was on fire, a change came over Malachi's wicked face.

He grinned. Then, he pointed one bony finger behind me. I turned. The finger pointed at a stopped vehicle, a shiny red mustang. Its owner must have been so proud of it, must have washed and waxed it every day. Now it sat all alone on a curb, thrown away and forgotten.

My feet stumbled of their own accord towards the car. Without urging, I screamed again and pounded my clenched fist against the window. There was no occupant, but it didn't matter. All the rage I had, it was all because of that car. That car was the reason for all of it. That car was why the Freeze happened. That car was why Mara froze. I hammered at the window and slammed my knee into the door with a crunch.

Other voices joined me, other disciples of rage battering their bodies into the car. Someone hurled a rock into the front window. The resulting cracks looked like the veins of a living animal that we had hunted, trapped, and would now consume. The back window shattered, leading to a chorus of gleeful shouts.

I joined in the shouting. It all made sense now – I was one of them. My hours and days of wandering were over. Two months trying to live life like things were still normal. And for what? Why dwell on the past when you can burn it instead?

The drum beat louder and louder. Malachi pointed to another car, then a storefront. The other Mad Ones and I shrieked and howled our way through clunkers and fast-food joints. The old world was dead and we were there to effect its forgetting.

Malachi pointed at a Sonic up ahead. The finger was pointed, our chaotic conductor had shown us the way, and as a horde we prepared to fling ourselves upon it.

Mara loved Sonic. She told me on our first date it was the only place in the world where you can get tater tots for dinner. To prove it, we went and got some right then and there.

I paused, fell out of step as the others rushed the Sonic. Rocks went through windows, bats and crowbars demolished the mounted speakers. Back in the parking lot, I simply stood still.

I used to shake when I got angry, when I remembered something that had happened, or when an off-handed comment set me off. And when she saw me shaking, Mara would reach out one steady hand and touch me in the middle of my back, right between my shoulder blades, to let me know she was there. For a moment I could feel her hand on my back, the whisper of her voice in my ear, as the Sonic in front of me was eaten up by flames.

The Mad Ones finished quickly, then progressed down the road. Malachi, marching to the beat of the drum, walked a few paces ahead of them. I remained.

Shaking my head, I went down the road in the other direction, walking towards my destination.

Pasado Lane Apartments looked just like it used to, as if it had been frozen in time years before the rest of the world. Its name was written in proud gold script against a red brick background. Two mighty oak trees formed a natural arch over the entrance. The grass leading up to the manager's office was overdue for a trim, but rather than looking sloppy, it gave the complex a warm, homey feel. As I followed the path to building D, my building, I slung my M4 over my back shoulder. I wouldn't need it here. I was safe now.

My breath quickened as I walked up the stairs to the second floor. My mind conjured up horrible images of what I might see. Then just like that I was there, standing in front of the door to Apartment 180. I brought my hand up to the doorknob and turned. It was unlocked.

After four hours of work, Apartment 180 looked exactly like it once did. I found a flat screen TV, a 32-inch Toshiba just like my old one, in Apartment 151. The owner had a hundred DVDs, so I brought ten to put on the stand underneath it. Then there was a Walmart coffee table in Apartment 132. The brown couch in Apartment 127 was a chore to get up the stairs by myself, but I managed. I even found a vanilla air freshener. Most importantly Apartment 176, just next door, had a bare metal folding chair that I carefully placed on the balcony, in the same spot where mine used to be, next to an upside-down plastic crate. The apartment was now set up just like that moment so many years ago.

Everything was ready. My spirit yearned in anticipation as I lay down on the couch. I willed my eyes to close.

My eyes opened. I sat up, then walked to the coffee table. I acted in a trance, as if part of a sacred rite. The air out on the balcony was cool and crisp, just like before. I reached down and lifted the pack of cigarettes off the crate. My hands trembled as I removed one cigarette from the pack and lit it. My first cigarette since I married Mara.

I breathed in deeply, the smoke passing into my lungs. I held it in for a second, and it felt like the whole frozen world around me was imprisoned in that lungful of air. Then with a sigh I breathed out, letting every care and trouble in my life exhale out into the air.

I felt nothing.

I tried it again. I breathed even deeper this time, willing my thoughts and memories to enter into my body so I could dispel them in a puff of smoke.

Again, nothing.

When I got back from the war and sat on the balcony, smoking a cigarette, I knew that everything was going to be okay. But now all I felt was nothing at all.

The trip back to my house went by without incident. I walked west on Montana and stayed in a different abandoned house overnight. I made my way up Mesa to Westwind. The Mad Ones and the lost nurse were nowhere to be seen, and I reached my house at the end of the second day. I unlocked the door and closed it gently behind me. I walked up the stairs to the bedroom.

Mara lay on the bed, still curled into a fetal position, hair spread out on the pillow like a halo. I wanted to touch her, to rub her back reassuringly to let her know I was there, just like she used to do to me. But I couldn't.

The day of the Freeze, Mara and I got in a fight.

"Why is this such a big deal?" I slammed my hand on the kitchen table.

Mara shuddered. "It's not a big deal, I just wanted to know how your day was."

I put my hands on my hips. "I spend all day putting up with people. Chris keeps bugging me about my reports, Vince wants me to come in this weekend, again, and all I want is one hour of peace and quiet to read, is that too much to ask?"

Mara picked up my book from the counter. "You want time to read?" She threw it into the living room. "Fine. Take the rest of your life."

Mara ran out of the kitchen. I heard steps pounding up the stairs.

"That's right, run away," I called out. "Every time things get even a little difficult, just run away."

The bedroom door slammed.

"You know, one of these days..."

And then it happened. A monstrous crash sounded all around and throughout the house, as if the sky itself had fallen onto the earth. Then the total and complete absence of sound.

That's how it happened. That's how the world froze.

I thought about all this as I looked down at Mara lying on the bed.

"Hey, it's me."

Mara didn't respond.

"I visited the old apartment, the one I lived in before we got married. It's just like it used to be."

Nothing.

I extended a hand and placed it on Mara's shoulder. Then, I lay down on the bed behind her.

"Mara, I've been thinking about what happened between us, about what I said." I gulped. "I'm sorry. I shouldn't have been angry at you, and I shouldn't have yelled. I should have just told you about my day."

Moments stretched into minutes.

"Did you hear what I said Mara? I said I'm sorry."

I sniffed. Then, I almost shouted. "I said I'm sorry! Aren't you going to say anything back?"

I paused, gritted my teeth to push it all down.

"You're supposed to say you forgive me, Mara. That was the deal we had, remember? When we got married, you told me that if I ever said I was sorry, you would forgive me."

Despite my best efforts, tears flowed out of my eyes. My arm wrapped around Mara as I buried my face into her amber hair.

"I'll do anything. I'll come home from work early, I'll never argue with you again. Just please, say something."

I stayed there until I ran out of tears. The warmth of Mara's unmoving body flowed out into my own, as the bed surrounded us in our very own cocoon of regret.

"Please Mara, just please say you forgive me."

Then I heard it. There was a noise, a rhythmic thud, coming from above me. Then all around. It took a moment to recognize it – it had been so long.

Outside, it was raining.

THE SHADOWBEAR COMETH!!!

(a tale of *woe* and *dread* in four parts)

Little children go to bed
Or a Shadowbear will touch your head
When you're touched again – oh no
Nobody knows where you go

Part 1 – The Den (in which I am touched by a SHADOWBEAR)

It all began on a scorching hot Saturday night in El Paso when I was trying to prove to my ex Yoli that I was over her, but instead ended up getting touched by a Shadowbear.

The air outside felt like a blow dryer on full blast. Nothing, and I mean nothing, was going to stop me from wasting Saturday night lounging on my black leather couch, A/C cranked to eleven, with a never-ending parade of ice-cold Coronas marching from the refrigerator into my mouth.

But then I checked my phone and saw that Yoli posted a photo of her, Taylor, and Denise (ugh, Denise), doing tequila shots at the Den. The Den! It would be one thing if Yoli did that at Cincinnati, or Hemmingway's, or Marco Polo, or even LBOT, but the Den? That was my place!

So what was I to do? I had no desire to actually see Yoli—it had only been two weeks since the break-up, still too early for a get back together hook-up—but if I stayed at home in my refrigerated air, drinking Corona, she was going to think I wasn't going out because she was out. She was going to think I wasn't over her!

I texted my boy Jerry. *Jerry. The Den. Now.*

Tiny bubbles. *Arent u chillin tonight?*

I was, but Yoli is at the Den.

Arent u avoiding Yoli?

Yeah, but I need her to see me at the Den so she doesnt know I'm avoiding her. [Angry face emoji] *CANT LET HER WIN.*

Busy. Sry.

Lame. Guess I'm flying solo. I walked to the Den and made it there in one piece, just a little sweaty from the heat. No biggie. It's only awkward if you let it be awkward. I sashayed through the main room to the back patio area where the soft glow of tiki torches lit up the bar. A kitschy chalkboard sign boldly proclaimed: "It's Island time, brah." A fake parrot hung from the eaves.

My eyes locked onto one seat, then another. Yoli wasn't there. Neither was Taylor, or Denise (and thank goodness, because I was not in a mood to handle Denise).

"Can I help you?" asked the bartender, sporting a red aloha shirt and sunglasses draped around his neck.

As a regular, it would be rude not to order.

"One Long Island, Chief. Easy on the sweet and sour."

Yoli wasn't at the Den. She also wasn't at Cincinnati, Hemmingway's, or Marco Polo. I didn't check LBOT because I would've had to Uber and, like, who has time for that? Defeated, I stumbled home. With each step I felt the Long Island from the Den, the rum and coke from Cincinnati, the whiskey and coke from Hemmingway's, and the vodka red bull from Marco Polo, sloshing around in my stomach.

I texted Jerry. *You know who's really hot, but no one ever talks about? Maid Marian in that Disney Robin Hood cartoon.*

Jerry texted back. *She was a fox.*

[Winky face emoji] *Yeah she was.*

Something blocked my path. The forward momentum of my stumbling pushed me smack into a solid wall of black matted fur. I grasped at the fur to steady myself.

An electric tingle jumped into my hand. I let go and stepped back. The tingle was already in my hand though, traveling up my arm throughout my body.

The solid wall of black fur shuffled around to face me. Seven feet tall and five hundred pounds, it was a mountain of pure muscle. Two colossal legs, each thicker than my entire body. Two humungous arms ending in sharp black claws. Fur so black it stood out against the night, blotting out stray stars that hazarded upon its vicinity. The face looking down at me was covered in fur as well. It opened its mouth wide, but instead of teeth, there was only darkness.

It was a Shadowbear.

I took another step back. The Shadowbear rolled its shoulders. With a smooth thrust, it reached out one claw. I stumbled. My right foot caught the seam of the sidewalk. Flimsy legs crumpled beneath me.

The Shadowbear towered above me. I pushed myself back with my hands. The cold concrete of the sidewalk scraped against my palms. The Shadowbear took one deliberate step forward. Its heavy foot boomed like a cannon as it crashed onto the ground.

Three point one miles per hour. I saw it in a documentary once, or maybe a commercial for a documentary before I shelled out the extra two dollars a month for the Hulu no commercials plan. Three point one miles per hour. That's how fast a Shadowbear can walk.

With a burst of adrenaline, I surged into a standing position and took off, racing back to my apartment.

I locked the door. Not that it would do any good. Shadowbears can walk through walls, everyone knows that. It was a mile back to my apartment, and I ran it in twelve minutes. Shadowbears go a mile in twenty minutes, so eight minutes until it would arrive. Right?

I called Jerry.

Ring. Ring. Ring. Ring.

Jerry eventually answered. "Bro, why can't you text like a normal person?"

"Jerry, bro, I just got touched by a Shadowbear."

"You're drunk, bro. That doesn't happen these days."

"I'm serious, bro. I got touched by a Shadowbear and I've only got eight minutes left, and that's, like, only if my math is correct, and I had a Long Island at the Den, rum and coke at Cincinnati, whiskey and coke at Hemmingway's, vodka red bull at Marco Polo, so I'm not, like, super confident in my math skills right now. Bro."

Pause. "Well get moving. Either that or disappear forever."

I dashed out the door without taking the time to lock it. In front of my apartment, my car slumbered underneath an overhang. At the other end of the parking lot, fifty yards away, stood the Shadowbear. Even from far away, its black fur sucked in all nearby light and consumed it without mercy.

I jumped behind the wheel of my car and turned the ignition. My heart beat so loud it drowned out the noise of the engine. I hit the accelerator, then slammed on the brakes.

The Shadowbear blocked my escape to the only exit as it plodded forward, one step at a time, at three point one miles per hour. The car idled with a low purr. The Shadowbear took a step closer, then another.

Now or never. I hit the accelerator and yanked the wheel to the right. As the car drifted past the Shadowbear, it stepped towards me. It reached out a single claw, and as I watched, the claw passed through my window and within an inch of my face.

Then I was past it, speeding away.

Safe.

For now.

Little children go to bed
Or a Shadowbear will touch your head
When you're touched again – oh no
Nobody knows where you go

Back in the day, I guess being touched by Shadowbears was somewhat common. You don't hear about it anymore, but everyone still knows the nursery rhyme – and the rules. Once a Shadowbear touches you, it will chase you until it touches you again. It'll walk over mountains, along the ocean floor, even through walls. And when it touches you again, you and the Shadowbear both disappear. Science claims to have all the answers, but even the brightest eggheads have no idea where you and the Shadowbear go.

Jerry once told me a story about an Indian who was touched by a Shadowbear. Hundreds of years ago, there was a young Indian warrior. He was out hunting buffalo, or whatever, when he looked up and saw a Shadowbear. He tried to roll out of the way, but the Shadowbear reached down and touched him.

The warrior ran back to his village. He went to the elders and was like, "Hey, I got touched by a Shadowbear. What do I do now?"

The elders were all like, "Yo, the tradition of our people is that once you are touched by a Shadowbear, you sit at the center of the village, in a teepee or whatever, and then the Shadowbear comes and touches you again and you go away. Or something like that."

But the warrior was all like, "Screw. That. I'm not sitting peacefully and waiting for the Shadowbear to touch me again and disappear. I'm a young brave warrior. I can run."

So the warrior started running. Each day he ran as far as he could. Then, while he slept, the Shadowbear got closer and closer, so the next day the warrior ran more. And to this day he still runs, always one step ahead of the Shadowbear. Cue dramatic music.

Part 2 – Running (from the SHADOWBEAR)

There were twenty-four miles of freeway between my apartment and my office, so I worked out a routine. Seven hours at home, then seven hours at work, then seven hours at home. Just as the Shadowbear reached me at one place, I would be on my way to the other. I tried to sleep when I was home, but the moment my eyes closed I saw the Shadowbear walking into my parking lot, plodding up the stairs to my apartment.

On the fourth day there was a knock at the door. My right hand gripped the couch's armrest tight enough to strangle it. Deep breath. It's okay. Shadowbears can walk through walls. They don't knock.

Behind the door stood a young woman in a black blazer, a clipboard clenched to her chest. Strands of jet black hair tried to escape from the tight bun in which they were imprisoned.

She looked down at the clipboard, pulling it away from her chest slightly to read it. "Mr. Ramiro?"

I nodded.

"Jessica Martinez, USAA Customer Service."

Her glasses were too big for her face. Her suit was a size too big as well, giving the impression of a young girl playing dress-up in her mother's clothes.

"May I come in?"

She sat down on the couch, in my seat. She crossed her legs, then crossed them in the other direction. She studied her clipboard.

"Good morning. I'm here today to discuss your options... no wait." She shook her head. "Get it together, Jessica." Inhale. Exhale. "I'm here today to discuss your policy. We express our deepest sympathy for your recent encounter with an *Ursus umbrus*, or 'Shadowbear.'" She made air quotes with her fingers. "USAA has been there for you during your life, and we are just as committed to being there for you during your death."

Realizing I was still standing, I sat down on a folding chair. "I don't have a USAA policy."

"Your life insurance policy, purchased by your parents at birth, contains a Shadowbear rider that allows you to collect half the amount of your life insurance, minus a small administrative fee, upon being touched by a Shadowbear."

A piece of paper was thrust into my hand. "Please initial here and here, "sign here, and you will receive a check for," Jessica checked her clipboard, "one hundred twenty thousand dollars. Minus a small administrative fee."

The sheet of paper stared up at me. I tried to read it. The font was two sizes too small. Also, should I be hitting on Jessica? Minus the oversized clothes, she was kind of cute, and she was already in my apartment. That meant steps one through six of my standard game plan were already mission complete.

My eyes focused in on one sentence. "What does 'alternate monthly payments' mean?"

Jessica cleared her throat. "The Shadowbear rider of your policy allows you, in lieu of a lump sum, to accept a reduced monthly payment for life. In your case, the monthly payment would be approximately ten thousand dollars."

"Minus a small administrative fee?"

"There's no administrative fee for the monthly option," Jessica said.

"Why not?"

Jessica looked to the left, then to the right. She leaned in slightly. "Because no one ever chooses it. Once you've been touched by a Shadowbear, you don't survive for more than a month. You get that, right? A Shadowbear doesn't eat, doesn't sleep, and doesn't stop. It plods ahead every minute of every day until it catches you."

I thought back to Jerry's story. "There's an old Indian tale of a man touched by a Shadowbear who spent his whole life running, and so managed to escape."

"I'm pretty sure that was a Twilight Zone episode, not an old Indian tale." Jessica took off her glasses and sighed. "Look, Mr. Ramiro. As an insurance and customer service professional, I recommend you take the lump sum option. Accept your fate."

I scribbled on the form and handed it back.

"I'd like my monthly ten thousand dollars. Please."

The knock on the hotel room door sounded like a stake being pounded into a coffin. I tensed, but only for a moment. Shadowbears don't knock. I buttoned the last button of my shirt. Too formal. I unbuttoned it. Shadowbear or no Shadowbear, I had to look good.

Jessica Martinez, USAA Customer Service, stood at the door with her clipboard.

"Mr. Ramiro, what a pleasure to see you again." She brushed past me into the hotel room. "I see Miami is treating you well."

She looked different. It took me a moment to figure it out.

"You're not wearing glasses anymore."

Jessica handed me an envelope. "Pursuant to the terms of your election, please accept this check."

I pulled the envelope out of her hand. "I opened a checking account with you guys. You could just direct deposit it."

"USAA policy requires me to hand you the check in person each month to verify that you are still alive. Also, Lasik."

"Lasik?"

"I got Lasik. So no more glasses."

"I see." I nodded towards the window. "I'm about to head out to the pool. They do a happy hour at five."

Jessica was looking at her clipboard again.

"You could join me if you want."

"What was that?"

"You could join me."

Jessica shook her head and gave a little laugh. "No, oh no. I'm not really a poolside happy hour kind of gal."

I shrugged. "Your loss."

The air outside was balmy and tropical. Two bars adorned in bamboo facades delivered a steady stream of complimentary drinks to those in attendance. Reggae covers of 80's one hit wonders played over the stereo. Most guests stood or sat in small circles of confidants, but one doe-eyed young co-ed sat by herself, staring into an artificial fire pit.

"Can I buy you a drink?" I asked, sitting down next to her.

"The drinks are free."

"In that case, can you buy me a drink?"

I botched the delivery, but the girl smiled anyways.

"You're the Shadowbear guy, aren't you?"

I nodded.

"I heard the receptionists talking. Is it true? You came to Miami to avoid being touched again?"

My right arm moved so it was not quite around the girl, but close enough to make it clear what was on my mind. "Guilty as charged."

The girl leaned forward, a sparkle in her eyes. "That's so exciting. Aren't you scared?"

"It's simple math. Shadowbears move at three point one miles per hour over land, but less than one mile per hour through water. There are one thousand, six hundred, and forty miles between El Paso and Miami, half of it through water. So it will take the Shadowbear forty-five days to get here. I've been here twenty-four days, so I can stay another fifteen, then fly to the west coast and start all over again."

The girl ate it up like I was some kind of math professor. "That's amazing, how you can calculate the exact time you have before it gets here."

It's called google maps. But I didn't say that. Instead I nodded and said, "I've got a gift for numbers."

"And it's amazing how you can take into account different routes." She inched closer until the fingertips of my right hand brushed against her tan shoulder. "I wonder what other gifts you have."

I jerked back a millimeter.

"What do you mean different routes?"

"Shadowbears always take the most direct route to get to their prey."

"Yes," I said. "And?"

"Since Shadowbears move slower in water, you must have taken into account whether a curved route that stayed on land the whole time, instead of a straight line that went through water, would bring the Shadowbear here faster."

The 80's reggae cover playing on the stereo shifted to a minor key. The shadows from the artificial fire pit grew deeper, colder.

The girl put one hand directly on my leg. "So, your room or mine?"

Twenty-five days. Assuming a Shadowbear goes from El Paso to Miami taking a land only route, it can get there in twenty-five days.

Bing. "Ladies and gentlemen, this is the Captain. We're going to be just a few more minutes."

My right foot tapped a rapid rhythm on the floor. "What is taking so long?" I pulled up the window shade, allowing the Miami sun to bathe my seat in golden light.

"I love the outside this time of year. It's simply marvelous."

I slammed the shade back down and looked at the old man sitting next to me. Middle seat, what a loser. Didn't he know there's an app for that?

"I like the indoors."

"I see," the old man replied. "Tell me young man, are you going on a trip or going home?"

This was stupid. The Shadowbear was there or it wasn't. Me opening the shade wouldn't change that. I opened the shade again.

It was there. Across an expanse of runway and a small grass field, the Shadowbear, MY Shadowbear, walked towards the plane at three point one miles per hour.

The plane beneath me rumbled.

Bing. "Thank you for your patience. We've been cleared for lift off."

As the plane crawled forward, the Shadowbear moved closer at the same pace. It was through the field of grass and onto the runway.

The plane picked up speed.

Bing. "This is an interesting tidbit, folks. If you look out the right hand side of the plane, you can see a Shadowbear walking down the runway."

The plane leapt into the air, abandoning the ground behind.

"Shadowbear, eh? I haven't seen one of those in years." The old man chuckled. "Little children go to bed, or a Shadowbear will—"

"It's not funny." Beneath my hand, the window shade slammed shut.

Another city. Another hotel room. Another knock on the door.

Jessica Martinez looked tired. So was I. I hadn't fallen asleep until well after the hotel bar closed.

"Good morning, Mr. Ramiro, may I please come in?" Jessica walked past me without waiting for a response.

We were in the sitting room portion of the two room suite. An assortment of empty bottles huddled on a desk. The couch cushions were piled in a tower next to the TV. No idea why. The door of the mini-fridge was wide open.

"It's been a while," I said.

"The execs saw how much it cost for me to fly out to see you, so they changed the requirement to once a year."

Perched on top of an office chair was a black negligee, which Jessica picked up using a pen and studied. "I see you've changed up your wardrobe."

"Very funny." I grabbed it away from Jessica and threw it on top of the couch cushion tower. When I looked back Jessica was holding out an envelope.

The bedroom door opened.

"Is that room service?"

"It's just a friend," I said over my shoulder. "She's leaving soon."

"Ask her if she's seen room service."

The door shut.

"Wow." Jessica folded her arms. "I didn't realize you brought your daughter with you."

"Haha, very funny," I said. "And she isn't that young. I met her at a bar."

"A juice bar?"

"Don't you have somewhere to be?"

Jessica let out an exaggerated sigh. "As a matter of fact I do. I woke up at two in the morning so I could fly here, give you your stupid money, and still make it home by this evening. My fiancée and I have our cake tasting."

"You're engaged?"

"Yes."

The sound of off-key singing wafted out of the bedroom.

Jessica raised an eyebrow. "Is she singing Taylor Swift?"

"Give her a break. It probably just reminds her of high school or something."

Jessica snorted. "I'm pretty sure she's still in high school."

"Is that your official USAA Customer Service opinion?"

"No. And I'm not in customer service anymore."

"You're not?"

Jessica shook her head. "I'm a manager on the finance side. However, company policy requires us to close out all cases from our previous assignment, so no matter where I go, I'm still responsible for your checks. As long as you're alive."

I looked down at the envelope. "Congratulations. On the promotion, and the engagement, and everything."

"Thank you."

The singing stopped.

Part 3 – Island Time (no SHADOWBEAR in this part)

I woke up on a couch. My eyelids stayed firmly shut, a futile attempt to guard my pounding head from the bright sunlight. Despite my lack of vision, I knew I was on a couch. And a cheap one at that. Lumpy padding, scratchy texture. The room had a moldy smell. Everything here did. It was just so humid that nothing ever completely dried.

I opened my eyes. A small boy, five or six, stared out of wide brown eyes as he sat cross-legged on a nearby coffee table. He startled at my stirring, then tilted forward.

"Are you my new daddy?"

A stern female voice came out of the next room. "Nico, leave the drunk man alone."

The boy scooted backwards, then jumped off the table and scampered out of the room. A woman marched in, holding a giant hamper full of unfolded clothes. She was a little on the chubby side, but had a nice face. I'd probably hit on her after a couple drinks.

I tried to sit up. "Hi, I'm—"

"I remember who you are." She plopped the laundry hamper on the floor. "I'm Dawn, in case you forgot. I'm assuming you forgot."

"Did that boy just ask—"

"He's messing with you, he asks everyone that."

The laundry at the top of the hamper was mine. The cognitive disconnect of seeing my clothes somewhere not on me made me aware that I was covered by a blanket, underneath which I was naked.

I fell back against the couch and pulled the blanket against my body. "Wait, did we—"

"In your dreams." Dawn was striding around the living room, pushing books and toys into their proper place. "Actually, not even in your dreams. I can only imagine what degenerate things you have going on in your head, and I want nothing to do with them."

Dawn paused her cleaning to glare at me. "Do you remember anything from last night?"

I shook my head.

"You don't remember getting drunk at Big Wave?"

Another shake.

"You don't remember me telling the cops I knew you so they wouldn't arrest you for public intoxication?"

That part sounded a little familiar.

"Thanks, I'll pay you back?"

"You can pay me back by folding the laundry." Dawn inclined her head towards the hamper, then walked back out of the room.

"Can I have an ibuprofen or something?"

"After you fold the laundry."

"Ugh, I'm dying here."

"You're not dying, you're just hungover. Deal with it."

I looked around. "With this kind of treatment, I am definitely not staying here a second night."

"If this was the last house on earth, you would not be staying here a second night."

"I'll get it!" Nico ran out of his bedroom, jumped over the couch, and grabbed the doorknob before I even noticed someone was knocking.

"Hello, lady," Nico said. "Are you my new mommy?"

Nico dashed away as Jessica stepped into the living room, wearing a white tank top with a colorful wrap around her waist. A purple flower balanced on her ear.

"Don't worry," I said. "He's just messing with you. He says that to everyone."

"Sorry I'm late. My records said you were staying at a hotel." Jessica handed me an envelope.

Dawn walked into the room. She made a circular wave with her open palm. "Hello, random lady inside my house."

Jessica reached out a hand. "Hi, I'm Jessica Martinez, Vice President of Corporate Finance, USAA."

"And you're here because…"

"Once a year I have to bring this guy his check."

Dawn took in Jessica's outfit. "Looks like you're enjoying your trip."

Jessica's face lit up. "I am. I brought my husband and kids, so we made a vacation out of it." She looked back at me, then at Dawn. "So are you two…"

"No," we said together.

"Sorry. I just thought, since you weren't at a hotel anymore."

I shook my head. Dawn said nothing.

"Well, I better get back. Who knows what Ron and the kids are up to." She turned to leave. "See you in a year."

Dawn turned off the light in Nico's bedroom, then crept into the living room. I removed the back cushions from the couch, placing them in their usual spot, and took my blanket out of the closet. The windows were open, letting a cool night breeze wend its way through the house. The lights in the living room were off, but there was enough ambient light coming through the windows to paint the interior in discernable shades of blue and gray.

Dawn stepped over a discarded toy and sat down beside me on the couch. There was a light scent of strawberries from the lotion she used every night before going to bed.

"You're thinking about him, aren't you?" Dawn whispered. "The one who chases you. I've never seen you this quiet."

I nodded my head. "I haven't been keeping count of how many days it's been since I arrived here."

"And that scares you, doesn't it?"

I exhaled. "It would take three months for a Shadowbear to get here from the west coast."

"You've been here almost that long."

Dawn was looking straight ahead, but I felt her attention on me. She had a way with her voice of letting me know she was fully focused on me even when she was cooking dinner, or grabbing Nico by the collar, or looking in another direction.

"Don't go," she said. There was a slight quiver in her voice. We weren't usually this serious, Dawn and I.

She said it again. "Please, don't go."

I shifted my weight on the couch. "The Shadowbear could be here tomorrow."

"You could get hit by a car tomorrow. I could get hit by a car. Our lives are just a mist. All we're promised is today."

That night I dreamt I was the Indian in Jerry's story. I was running and running, except in the dream the Shadowbear could run too. I ran through wooded paths, parched deserts, and windy beaches, and wherever I ran the Shadowbear followed. I ran until my calves froze like concrete and my lungs could hold no more air. Then the Shadowbear's breath fell onto the back of my neck.

I left a note, even though I knew Dawn would never read it. I left the window shade open as the plane went faster and faster along the ground, at last soaring up into the sky. I didn't see the Shadowbear out the window this time, but I knew it was out there, searching. And it would never stop until it found me.

Part 4 – The End

From that day forward, I never stayed anywhere more than a week. I took my monthly insurance check and invested it wisely. Before long, I had condos all over the world and rotated among them so the Shadowbear was always at least one time zone away. Until now.

"That's quite a story," Jessica said.

"You were there for most of it."

Jessica's hair had finally lost its battle with time. It was fully gray, as was mine. She still moved with grace, but like me, it took her a little longer to stand up or sit down.

"So why now?"

Resting my elbows on the arms of my chair, I folded my hands in front of my chest. "Once we're done, what are you going to do?"

Jessica's eyes sparkled. "My eldest granddaughter is graduating from high school at noon, and I wouldn't miss it for the world."

"And how about your job? I heard they're going to make you CEO."

A little laugh. "It's not certain. I might retire."

My hands dropped into my lap. "Grandchildren. CEO. Not bad for a scared young lady who used to hide behind her clipboard."

"That's life. You mature, you grow up."

"Do you? A couple years ago, they made this movie about my life."

"*The Shadowbear Cometh*," Jessica said. "I remember. It made me a bit of a celebrity around the office. I didn't like the actress who played me though."

"They tried to make it all dramatic and exciting, but when I actually saw my life story up on screen, it all seemed so… pointless." I paused. "All these years I was trying to stay alive, but I don't think my life ever actually began. I'm ready for that now though. Ready to start my life."

From the door of the hotel room came three deliberate knocks.

"I believe that's my cue." I rose to my feet.

Jessica looked confused. "It's knocking? That's impossible. Shadowbears can walk through walls. They don't knock."

I smiled. "I once thought that too." I moved towards the knocking.

"Where do you think it takes you?" Jessica asked, a subtle shade of concern in her voice.

I stopped and stood there a moment. "I haven't the faintest idea." My shoulders shrugged of their own accord. "It must be somewhere wonderful though. After all, no one ever comes back."

My feet took one step at a time towards the everlasting knock that would never cease until I stopped ignoring it. My hand grabbed the doorknob. Deep breath.

I opened the door.

Running

Night blankets the world around her. She runs through deserted city streets, and the Hunter follows close behind.

"Run… run… run… safe!"

Sophomore year, her father went to every single one of her track meets, even the away ones. During the sixteen hundred, he would stand at the finish line and yell as she got closer.

"Run… run… run…" and then right as she crossed the finish line, "safe!"

The next year they passed the Registration Act, and father wasn't allowed on school grounds anymore. But she still imagined his voice during every meet, as she got closer and closer to the end.

"Run… run… run… safe!"

She doesn't know how long she's been running. There was a time before she ran, she knows that, but it seems unreal now. Like a dream. This, what she's doing right now, this is real. The warm night air around her. The stink of sewage emanating from each dumpster she passes. The impact as her feet hit the sidewalk. The strain in her lungs as she gasps for air between each stride. The thud of the Hunter's boots, running behind her. This is right now. This is real.

The Hunter's boots grow louder. He's gaining on her. She pictures her body as a bank full of speed, just like her track coach taught her. Every time she trains, that's making a deposit of speed in the bank. Then, when she needs to, she can make a withdrawal.

She makes a withdrawal, and she sprints, shooting away like an arrow released from a bow. The Hunter's footsteps recede behind her. But next time, will she have enough? Does the bank have any speed left?

How did this all start? That's right. Just three months ago, in Seattle, while she was running. It was night of course. She never ran during the day. Even though high school track was behind her, she still liked to run. It cleared her mind, helped her think. Halfway through her usual five-mile route around her college's campus, she stopped. A large yellow sign hung on the door of the Night Children friendly church she had been going to since she moved there. She walked up to the old wooden church door, pulling earbuds out of her ears. The last song in her running playlist faded into nothingness. She had to see what the yellow notice said.

"Hey hot stuff, what are you doing all alone at this time of night?"

His breath reeked of alcohol. The strong, cheap stuff. She ignored him and kept reading.

"What's the matter, why so serious?" He touched her shoulder. He shouldn't have done that.

She whipped around and hissed, mouth opening wide as her canines slid out of their sheaths. It wasn't intentional, just pure fight or flight instinct, but that didn't stop the man from jumping ten feet in the air.

"Hey, chill out! Just trying to be friendly."

As the creep scampered off, she turned back to read the yellow notice on the door of the church. It was addressed to people like her, telling them to report for relocation. The day had finally come. Father had been wrong after all.

Father was always an optimist. That's why he came to all her track meets, before the Registration Act, and cheered her on at each one as if she might actually win. When she first started to run track, a group of parents circulated a petition saying she should be banned because she had an unfair biological advantage. They said "the science" showed her metabolism made her run faster. Idiots. Everyone knows Night Children are stronger and faster at night, but that running in the daylight saps the energy from them. She had to work twice as hard as any other girl on that team. But she did.

Like all Night Children, she had to wear sunscreen during the day to stop her skin from burning. Whenever she ran though, she sweated, and the sunscreen started to run. By the end of each race she could feel patches of her skin begin to cook. But she couldn't be distracted by that. Focus on the race.

Father set up a small camping tent and pitched it right next to the finish line. The moment she crossed, she could jump into the tent, away from the sun, and slap salve on the welts where the sunscreen came off completely. She thought about that tent each time she approached the finish line.

"Run…" She was in the home stretch. "Run…" Just a little closer, the sun searing her skin. "Run…" Almost there, the pain threatening to overwhelm her. "Safe!" She crossed the finish line and into the waiting embrace of the tent's shade.

The sprint, her withdrawal from the speed bank, worked. For a moment she's free. She can barely hear the Hunter behind her. Before the Hunter can catch up again, she darts into a short alley, then makes a right turn when she's out of it, moving in the direction opposite from where she had been going. Hopefully it's enough to throw the Hunter off.

When she reaches another alley she ducks into it and stops. She's flattened against the wall. She wills her body to be still and silent, but the heaving of her lungs overwhelms her ears like a freight train. The Hunter's boots grow louder, then softer as they go past her hiding spot. She's safe. For now.

She sinks to the ground. It's been a week since she's fed, and it's catching up to her. Far away a siren makes its way across the city. She lies down. Just for a moment. Just long enough to catch her breath.

Footsteps wake her up. Crap, she fell asleep. She can sense a man walking close to her, to where her body is curled into a fetal position against the alley wall. She pretends she's still asleep. He walks by. She breathes out.

The footsteps stop. Start to get louder again. The man has turned around and is walking back towards her. The man stops. He squats on the ground, bending his head down to be near hers. He's not going to go away.

Her eyes snap open. She raises her head and tries to hiss, but she falls back down to the ground almost immediately. She looks up into his brown eyes and it hits her.

I know him.

The brown eyed boy was in her chemistry class in tenth grade. That's how they first met. Her parents sent her to a public school in Portland, even though it meant she was one of only three Night Children in the entire class. She begged them to go to an alternative school, one for people like her, but they wouldn't listen. Father was an optimist after all. He said someday they would be accepted, and that "mainstreaming" her now was the best guarantee for her to succeed later in life. She was going to go to Harvard someday, she was going to be a doctor, or a lawyer, or a senator, and nothing she said could convince her father otherwise.

On the first day of chemistry Mr. Germaine scoured the class from behind oversized second-hand glasses. "Is there anyone willing to be Sundara's partner? Anybody?"

His gaze fell on Becky, sitting at the desk next to her. Becky was checking something on her phone and looked up when she realized the whole class was starting at her.

Becky put her phone down on the desk. "You see, Mr. Germaine, I would, except what if I cut myself on lab equipment and then Sundara, like, feeds on me?"

The class laughed. Mr. Germaine rapped his knuckles on his desk.

"Settle down. That's not funny."

"Exactly, it's not," Becky muttered, just loud enough for her to hear.

She turned towards Becky and hissed, canines coming out of their sheaths. Becky recoiled.

"That's enough, Sundara," Mr. Germaine said. "Don't bare your teeth in class, you know the penalty."

"Mr. Germaine, I'll be Sundara's partner."

The voice belonged to a brown eyed boy sitting on the other side of her. He had floppy hair that obscured one eye and wore a black coat that was already out of fashion when he bought it.

Mr. Germaine nodded and jotted down something in his notebook. The brown eyed boy turned to her and smiled.

She looked around to see if anyone was watching, then turned back to the brown eyed boy. "Are you trying to hit on me?"

The brown eyed boy shrugged. "I heard you were smart. I'm just trying to find a smart lab partner I can cheat off of."

"Well you can forget whatever you read about Night Children in your freaky fetish internet chat rooms, because it's not true."

She snorted and turned back to the front of the classroom, where Mr. Germaine was writing out equations on the white board.

That was the year a starving Night Child went blood crazy at a McDonald's in San Antonio and drained three children before the police put him down. A week later, another Night Child killed four people on a Los Angeles subway during the morning commute.

There was a march on Washington, angry people holding up signs saying "enough was enough" and begging the government to do something. The news ran stories about the attacks all day and all night. Commentators shook their heads at how we were the only civilized country where this sort of thing happened on a regular basis, opining that we shouldn't let Night Children just walk around on the street without common sense limitations. That's when the Registration Act got passed.

The smell of blood wakes her. She's lying on a couch, under a loose blanket. The brown eyed boy sits on a folding chair next to the couch. He's holding his arm out in front of her face. There's a slash down his forearm. The razor blade that made it lays discarded on a side table. Blood is oozing out of the cut, its sweet scent drawing her out of sleep's warm embrace into a state of semi-wakefulness.

"Come on Sundara, you need this," he says. "You've gone too long without feeding. I can see it in your eyes."

She shakes her head. It's not right. She's not a savage like her ancestors, this is not how she feeds. But the brown eyed boy continues to hold his forearm just before her lips.

Everything takes effort. She opens her mouth, and the canines shyly poke out of their sheaths. When she can feel them fully extend, she contracts her abdomen, raising her upper body that final inch. Then she buries her teeth into his flesh and starts to drink.

Towards the end of senior year, one of the popular girls, probably Becky, left a syringe full of blood on her desk in AP US History. She returned from a bathroom break and had halfway sat down when she saw it. She could tell from the smell it wasn't human. Probably pig or cow. Beneath it someone wrote "*bon appetit*" in chalk. She turned around and ran into the hallway.

She couldn't let them see her cry. Couldn't let them win. She started running down the hall because that's what she always did. Run. Get away. Clear her head. She wasn't in a track meet, and it had been two years since father had been allowed onto school property, but she could still hear his voice.

"Run... run... run..."

At the end of the hallway the brown eyed boy stood by a water fountain, looking up at the sound of her footsteps. She steered into him and collapsed crying into his arms.

"Safe."

The large yellow notice on the church, and the copies reprinted in every newspaper, directed all Night Children to report to their hometowns for initial processing. So she left her college in Seattle and went back to Portland. The day before the report date, she met her father at Little John's. It had been her favorite restaurant growing up. Sure, blood was blood, but some restaurants did a better job of letting you feel normal when they served it, while others made you feel like a freak. It was day, so she wore a long overcoat and a hat, sunscreen guarding the few exposed pieces of skin.

"Sundara, you came," her father said, standing to greet her as she approached his table. He grabbed her wrists with his hands, as she did the same to him, and they touched foreheads before they sat down.

She smiled. "Of course, father."

Father nodded. His hands were folded in front of him, but he kept fidgeting, eyes darting around the few other customers.

"Sundara, I spoke to friends of mine in the government, old friends, and I do not think you should report."

She tilted her head. "We have to report. We've been ordered. For our own safety if nothing else."

Father gritted his teeth. "Sundara, I do not know where they are going to take us, but I do not think it is somewhere safe."

He inclined his head down, towards a backpack on the floor next to his feet.

"Everything you need is in there. Money, IDs, blood for a week."

She looked around, but the other customers paid them no attention, too wrapped up in their own lives to notice anything out of the ordinary.

"And what do I do with it?" She swallowed.

Father leaned in close to her ear. His lips moved, words pouring out at a bare whisper. "Run, Sundara. Run as fast and as far as you can, and never look back. Go south, towards Mexico. Run until you are safe."

He looked around, another visual sweep of the restaurant. "The government has hired Hunters to track down any of us who do not report tomorrow. Real Hunters, with crossbows, just like in the old days. They will be on the lookout tonight for anyone who is running, so you need to leave today, before they expect you to."

Father used his foot to push the backpack closer to her.

"Take it, Sundara. Run. Live."

She reached down and grabbed the backpack. It was heavier than it looked, but she was in shape. She had trained for this.

"Farewell, father."

"Farewell, Sundara."

Throwing the backpack over her shoulder, she left the restaurant. And then she started running.

For the second time she wakes up in the brown eyed boy's apartment. She's still tired, but she feels strength from his blood running through her body.

The brown eyed boy is in a recliner. Head leaned back. Fast asleep. He looks older now than he did in high school, of course so does she. His hair is cut close to his scalp, and he has a day's worth of stubble on his face. His wrist is bandaged where she fed on him.

He's not going to wake up for an hour at least, not after losing that much blood. She starts to look around his apartment. It's small, but he's made the most of the space. She can't imagine how he ended up here, in a small border town over a thousand miles from where they grew up. He once told her that he wanted to leave Portland, but she didn't think he'd go this far.

For a man, he has a lot of decorations in the small apartment. There's a forest landscape, just like the woods outside their school, above a small particle board dining room table. A set of three matching abstract canvases cover the wall next to the door. On the side table next to his recliner is a framed photo. She leans in closer, mindful not to bother him.

It's the two of them, at prom. She forgot they went to prom together. But he hadn't. He kept this photo with him, on his long journey down here.

She looks around, and she starts to wonder.

"Run until you are safe." That's what father said. But she was never really safe. Not in college in Seattle. Not in high school in Portland. But standing here in this apartment, she doesn't have to run anymore. She can spend Friday nights watching Netflix and Sunday mornings sleeping in before making separate breakfasts. Omelet for him, blood for her. They won't reminisce about high school. She wants to leave all that in the rearview mirror, although she'll let him keep the prom photo if he insists. Instead they'll make new memories, new inside jokes that they can someday look back on and laugh at.

And then one day she'll come home with groceries, at night of course, and there will be a Hunter standing over the brown eyed boy, emptying bullet after bullet into his body. Then the Hunter will drop his gun from one hand as he removes the crossbow from his back with the other. He will load a bolt, charge the handle, aim at her. Pull the trigger.

She puts down the prom photo. She didn't realize she had picked it up. The brown eyed boy, really a man now, is still sleeping. She touches his face with her hand, and he twitches in his sleep.

This apartment is indeed a safe place. But only for him. She grabs her backpack and walks to his door. When she gets to the door, she will pause for a moment, but just a moment, so she can touch the doorframe. She won't turn back as she leaves.

She doesn't know how long she's been running. The precious hours she spent in the brown eyed boy's apartment are a dream. This, this is real. The burning in her lungs and her legs, the jarring impact of her soles against the pavement, is all real.

The Hunter's boots get louder, but she pays no attention, because she's made it. She's at the foot of the bridge going over the Rio Grande and into Mexico. There's no traffic. It's the middle of the night. She ignores the closed pedestrian walkway and starts running up the middle of the vehicle lanes. The Hunter's footsteps follow her.

Every muscle screams at her to stop, to rest, even if just for a moment.

The crest of the bridge, the actual border, is just twenty yards away. An American flag and Mexican flag mark where one country ends and another begins. Behind her comes the mechanical crank of the Hunter charging the handle of his crossbow. She reaches deep inside her speed bank and withdraws everything she still has there.

"Run…"

She's on the final stretch.

"Run…"

She's sprinting down the hallway of her high school and the brown eyed boy is waiting for her, arms open, next to the water fountain.

"Run…"

As she crosses the finish line she stumbles, but she stumbles into the brown eyed boy's arms.

"Safe."

Circles

It was nine a.m. in the third circle of Los Angeles, and Ricky Salazar was just three sales away from being able to see sunlight. Standing behind his fish cart, Ricky rewarded himself with the luxury of a ten second daydream.

The fritzy neon sign for the strip club on the other side of the street cast an intermittent orange glow on the third circle denizens walking below it. Ricky pretended he was up on the second circle, and the light from the neon sign was the warm sunlight passing through street grates above. The second long gaps when the neon sign went dead were clouds passing in front of the sun. The hum of the video screens in the shop next to him were the polite conversations of genteel second circle residents. The smell of the nearby alley—spilled beer mixed with dried urine—was the briny scent of the seashore, wafting down from the surface.

A middle-aged man in a light gray suit, an old overstuffed briefcase underneath his arm, approached Ricky's cart. The daydream ended. The man had slicked back dirty blonde hair and straight white teeth, like a politician or a movie star.

"Good morning, friend. I'm Harvey Goodfellow, counselor at law, civil rights attorney extraordinaire. Any chance I could trouble you for a tilapia?"

Ricky's cart consisted of two large tanks of water with a cutting board and small storage area on top of them. The bottom tank was empty while the top one held an angry looking fish almost as big as the tank itself.

"I have a catfish all grown and ready to go. Can I interest you in a catfish?"

Harvey Goodfellow, counselor at law and civil rights attorney extraordinaire, wrinkled his nose and shivered. "God no. I don't eat catfish, they're nothing but bottom feeders. Do you know what that means?"

Ricky shook his head.

Harvey looked around conspiratorially, then leaned in and whispered into Ricky's ear. "It means they eat other animals' poop. That's what it means."

Ricky shrugged. "I can grow you a tilapia, but it will take five minutes. That okay with you, sir?" He added the "sir" because Harvey Goodfellow looked like an important person, and Ricky had learned that sometimes important people like it better, and give you better social media reviews, if you call them "sir."

Harvey tilted his head and looked off into the distance, checking the time using his implants. "I can do five minutes."

Ricky reached into his bag of pellets and grabbed a tilapia. They were color coded, but Ricky didn't bother looking. Different pellets had different feels to them, like recognizing someone by their voice. After so many years in the fish business, Ricky could tell the difference.

The pellet was inserted into the feeder tray for the bottom tank. It was a bit sticky, but Ricky jammed it shut with ease. A few twists of the dials and knobs later, electricity was shooting through the bottom tank where the small pellet was wriggling and growing.

Ricky took out his filleting knife and began to sharpen it. Twenty-degree angle against the whetstone. Drag once, drag twice, then flip over. Drag again.

Without warning the video screens in the shop next door turned an ominous red. A voice clanged out from speakers placed throughout the street. If Ricky had implants, he would have been able to hear the message inside his head, but all he had was an old-fashioned phone, so he had to listen with his ears.

"Warning, civil unrest in progress," the voice proclaimed. *"Remain indoors. Follow all law enforcement instructions. Warning, civil unrest in progress."*

Harvey Goodfellow jumped in place, then peered into nothingness with his implants.

"My God, they set him free." Harvey shook his head.

"Set who free?"

Harvey gestured in the air, towards the screen of data his implants were showing him.

"Officer Lance Jones. Don't you follow the news? Officer Jones is the one who shot that black boy a few weeks back. He did it in cold blood, and they just set him free." Harvey exhaled with a humph. "Just goes to show some lives don't mean anything in this world."

The sound of shouts and breaking glass drifted over from down the street. Harvey looked around. "I have to go."

"But your tilapia – it's almost done!"

"No time for that now." Harvey pointed down the street. "You hear the sound of those rioters? They're just as angry about this verdict as I am, and you don't want to be around when they get here."

Ricky put the filleting knife down and planted his feet. He looked up at Harvey. "I already put the pellet in, sir, and the tilapia is almost grown. I need that money. You can't just walk off without paying."

Harvey narrowed his eyes. "Forget the money, those people coming down the street will wreck your cart and heave you halfway through death's door. You need to run while you can."

Ricky looked around. The strip club across the street showed no signs of closing, but the owner of the shop next to him was lowering a rugged steel grate across the storefront. With a protesting creak, the steel grate stopped moving a third of the way down. The owner tugged at the chain, but it wouldn't budge.

Harvey rummaged around his briefcase and pulled out a red hat with bold white lettering.

"This is a limited-edition Peoples United hat. I got it at a march years back. If you wear it, the rioters might leave you alone, might assume you're one of them." Harvey held it out a few inches from Ricky's face. "It's yours for twenty dollars."

Ricky pushed the hat away. "I need my money to get to the second circle. If you're not going to pay for your fish, you can just take your hat and leave."

While Harvey scampered off, Ricky took stock of his situation. He now had two full grown fish filling up both his tanks. Sigh. No more custom orders until he sold those two.

The sound of shouting grew louder. There was something else, a dull burning scent that smelled the way a nosebleed tastes, making its way through the poorly vented thoroughfares of the third circle.

The strip club sign on the other side of the street fritzed, then went out entirely. That wasn't good.

Ricky normally avoided alleys, no one ever goes in an alley to look for fish, but today might be an exception. Pulling up on one side of the cart so it balanced on its two wheels, Ricky started pushing it into a nearby alley.

A rough hand pawed at Ricky from behind. He would have fallen, but the cart steadied him. Ricky spun around to face his assaulter.

There were three of them, three men facing him from the other side of his cart. They wore matching black scarves over the lower halves of their faces, but that was where their resemblance to each other ended. The first was tall, much taller than Ricky, with short curly hair as dark as the black pulp Ricky fed to his fish to keep them happy once they were grown. The second man was short, almost comically so, with unkempt brown hair that covered his eyes and skin as white as tilapia flesh. The third man, bald, was of medium height, about eye to eye with Ricky.

The tall man spoke first. "Are you seriously selling fish? On a day like this?"

Ricky focused his attention on the speaker, but kept his eyes scanning in case one of the other two tried something.

"I sell fish every day," Ricky said. "It's how I make a living."

The short man with messy brown hair kicked the cart, not hard enough to tip it over, but enough to show his displeasure with the answer.

"While you try to make a living, other people are just trying to live."

The short man kicked the bottom tank again. The tank's resident, a now fully-grown tilapia, pressed its mouth against the glass where the kick had landed.

"Don't do that," Ricky said. He made eye contact with each of the three men as he said it.

A chair went through the window of the shop next door, spilling glass all over the street. A couple shards landed at Ricky's feet.

"Warning, civil unrest in progress. Remain indoors. Follow all law enforcement

instructions. Warning, civil unrest in progress."

The bald man stepped forward, grabbing the fish cart with both hands. "You don't care about your fellow man, do you? One of our brothers has been shot dead in the streets by the cops, and you don't care one lick about him."

Ricky stepped up to the cart, placing both hands on it so he was the mirror image of the bald man. "I care about getting to the second circle. All I need is three more sales, and then I can afford the transit fee. That's what I care about."

The bald man shook his head. He turned as if to leave, then slammed his foot into the bottom tank. The small crack from the impact spread through the glass like a bolt of lightning filling up the sky. With a violent gush, the contents of the tank, tilapia and all, spilled out onto the street.

The filleting knife was already in Ricky's hand. Ricky couldn't remember how it got there, or why. Usually he only picked up the knife when he was getting ready to prepare a fish.

It seemed so natural, as the bald man pulled back his foot for another kick, to thrust the knife into his chest. It felt very different than chopping the head off a fish. That sticking feeling might be a bone, a human bone, way tougher than fish ones. And the amount of blood was all wrong, way more than there should be.

"Warning, civil unrest in progress. Remain indoors. Follow all law enforcement instructions. Warning, civil unrest in progress."

Ricky sat in a black room, surrounded by panels of glass, lit from above by a bank of white fluorescent lights. It reminded him of a phone booth from the movies. It was cold, which was good because Ricky was feeling a bit sleepy. He couldn't remember how long he had been awake.

A metallic voice came out of an unseen speaker.

"Good morning. I am Legal Analysis Unit 1783, and I have been assigned to adjudicate the case of the People versus Ricardo Salazar. You have been charged with homicide by stabbing in the course of civil unrest. How do you plead?"

Ricky looked around, but couldn't see where the voice was coming from. Everything was black, no decorations or anything else that would let him get his bearing.

"Sorry, who are you?"

Pause. "I am Legal Analysis Unit 1783. I am a non-sentient artificial intelligence construct, programmed to dispense equal justice without bias with regards to race, ethnicity, national origin, sexual identity, or sexual orientation."

Ricky swallowed. "So you're a robot."

"I am not a robot," the voice replied. "Robots have physical bodies. I have no physical body. I am a non-sentient artificial intelligence construct, programmed to dispense equal justice..."

Ricky tuned out the rest.

"How do you plead?"

Ricky bit his lip. "I'm not sure. I guess innocent?"

The digital voice sounded indignant. "So you deny committing homicide by stabbing in the course of civil unrest?"

"Well, I did it, but I didn't mean to kill the guy. I was just trying to protect my fish cart."

"So your fish cart is worth the life of a man?"

Ricky shook his head. "It's not that at all. It's just, I need my fish cart to make money, and I almost have enough money to get to the second circle."

The voice boomed out. "Why do you want to go to the second circle?"

Ricky rubbed his chin. He opened his mouth, then closed it, then opened it again.

"The first circle is outside, with sunlight and fresh air and all that. Sure, that would be great, but maybe it would be too much for me. But you see in the first circle they have these grates on the street, for water and trash and the like. Sunlight goes through these grates, so in the second circle, when you walk around, there are beams of sunlight streaming down, striking the ground with a golden glow directly beneath the grates. That's all I want. To see the sunlight."

The room was silent when Ricky finished. Ricky imagined the robot thinking about what he said. He didn't wait long.

"Based on your confession, as corroborated by eyewitness testimony, I find you guilty of homicide by stabbing in the course of civil unrest. The penalty is death. Goodbye."

The glass chamber filled with electricity, just like one of Ricky's fish tanks. Ricky screamed as his flesh burned and the world dissolved around him.

It was almost noon in the third circle of Los Angeles, and Derrick Smith was pretty sure he would never see the sunlight. The customer in front of him, a well-dressed lawyer named Harvey Goodfellow, tapped his foot impatiently while Derrick smacked the bottom tank of his fish cart, willing the tiny salmon inside to grown faster.

It was the electro-stimulator, that had to be it. Or maybe something was wrong with the feed packet? If it was the electro-stimulator, where on earth was he going to get the money for a new one?

A mechanical voice cut across his thoughts. *"Warning, civil unrest in progress. Remain indoors. Follow all law enforcement instructions. Warning, civil unrest in progress."*

Harvey Goodfellow shook his head. "Did you hear? They just

announced the execution of Ricky Salazar, that fishmonger who killed the boy during the riot. He was just trying to defend himself though, it's a crying shame. Just goes to show there's no justice in this world for people like us."

From down the road came the ominous sound of raised voices and breaking glass. Derrick looked around, trying to find a place to stash his fish cart.

Harvey Goodfellow opened his briefcase, rooted around, then pulled something out.

"This is a limited-edition Peoples United hat. I got it at a march years back. If you wear it, the rioters might leave you alone, might assume you're one of them."

The man held it out a few inches from Derrick's face. "It's yours for twenty dollars."

trance

They met in a club called *New Eden*. This was back in 2001, when there were still actual trance clubs in Los Angeles (not just normal clubs that play trance music, serve expensive drinks, and hope no one can tell the difference). And this was back when actual ravers went to these clubs, not just exiles from hip-hop clubs who would come to stare at the few remaining candy kids like they were penguins in a zoo.

Dorian was a glowsticker. He was one of the self-chosen few that would show up to raves and trance clubs, glowsticks in hand, and take part in an intricate dance that would captivate all those who watched. The pervasive ecstasy and ketamine use among the constituents of these clubs made the captivation easier. Dorian came to watch Yoshi, a recent arrival from San Francisco, who was at *New Eden* to promote a glowsticking battle he was hosting the next weekend at *Circus Disco* (a club just down the block). Maria came because it was a Friday night, and she was a freshman at USC, and going to clubs is what she did on Friday nights when she was a freshman. There were a lot of Friday nights that year.

Maria never would've noticed Dorian, except that on that night he had foregone his trademark two aqua colored glowsticks for an orange and a blue. From deep inside an ecstasy-induced fog, Maria saw the dancing orange and blue lights and was momentarily propelled back to the year before, to high school, when they had given orange and blue pom-poms to all the students for homecoming. Orange and blue were her high school's school colors.

Sweat pouring like a waterfall out of the back of her head, Maria pushed herself up out of the corner of the trance room, out of range of the hipster who was giving her a back-rub, and through the crowd until she was just a few feet away from where Dorian was glowsticking. William Orbit's cover of *Adagio for Strings* was playing in the background, and Maria walked in time to the beat. She thought the dancing lights were very, very pretty. Dorian thought Maria was the most beautiful girl he had ever seen.

Dorian learned to glowstick in high school from his older brother. His older brother, a tennis player, had taken up glowsticking in order to become more agile. Dorian started because he thought it would be an easy way to impress girls. Every day he did three hundred helicopters with each hand in front of the mirror, spinning each glowstick in a circle and catching it with ease, constantly critiquing his own form. He did two hundred vertical flips, fifty double helicopters, and fifty full boxes.

Soon, glowsticking became more than just a way to impress girls: it was an art, a purpose. Dorian surpassed his brother's skill level and was forced to seek knowledge elsewhere. He joined countless web forums and learned the newest moves from 120x240 streaming video on websites with names like "www.glowstickersRpeople2.com" and "www.ravers4christ.org." Around the time Dorian started to get really good, the battlers began to emerge.

A normal glowsticker (a "true" glowsticker they would argue) could dance by himself, waiting for a circle of E-tards (those who had taken enough ecstasy to permanently alter their brain chemistry) to gather around and gape in amazement. For true glowstickers it was all about the art, the unity, the spirit of PLUR.

The battlers were looking for something different. They staged elaborate competitions in which one glowsticker would face off against another to prove their worth through a neon-colored twist on ancient combat. The skills that usually seemed so impressive were matched up with skills that were just as good.

Dorian believed all actions of all people were motivated by the desire to connect. He told this to Maria while sitting at a table in The Pantry Café (located at the corner of 9th and Figueroa and open 24 hours a day) as she was coming down from an unusually long ecstasy trip at *New Eden*.

"Every time a human being comes into contact with another," he explained, "a connection is formed. Sometimes they're small connections and sometimes they're big. Sometimes positive, sometimes negative. But they're all connections."

Maria wondered what kind of drugs Dorian did. She believed you could tell a lot about a person based on the types of recreational materials in which he engaged. After much deliberation, she decided Dorian seemed like a DXM guy. Even though, as Maria would later find out, Dorian never touched illegal substances, she continued to think of him as a DXM guy for a long time to come.

"That's why people are afraid of death," Dorian continued, "because they think that when they die, they lose all those connections. If they only understood the truth."

Maria didn't know what he meant. She did not understand.

Maria was afraid of death because when she was five, her dad sat her on his knee and promised (in a voice only a five-year-old could believe) that he would never leave her. Maria never made promises because she worried she couldn't keep them.

Maria's first boyfriend was a meth dealer named Fahad, who was taking classes at Pierce Community College (part-time) while trying to break into the DJ business. When they first met (it was 80's night at a club called *The World* at Hollywood and Sycamore), he told her she looked like Jaci Velasquez, except flatter. Maria found this very tactless. Two weeks later, at Fahad's insistence, she tried ecstasy for the first time. They broke-up a few months later when Fahad found Jesus and enrolled at Biola University. Fahad later became a youth pastor and used Maria (under a pseudonym, of course) as a classic story to tell to "at risk youth." He even wrote the story down in a book, which sold quite a few copies, and made Fahad quite rich. However, he donated all the proceeds to a Christian anti-ecstasy organization called "raverz4christ."

At an annual rave called *March Madness* (it took place at some roller skating rink in San Dimas), Dorian was putting on an especially good show for a circle of appreciative candy kids when Yoshi arrived.

Yoshi's arrival was heralded by the excited screaming of several attendees, both candy kids and glowstickers. He had his own posse, fellow battlers who followed him around in an effort to emulate his style.

"Are you here to battle?" he said to Dorian, the very question itself a challenge.

"I'm here to glowstick," Dorain replied.

"You can't fool me," said Yoshi. "I'm the best glowsticker in Los Angeles, probably in the world. It's okay to admit you're afraid of losing to me."

Dorian was quiet. He turned to Maria, who in turn was talking to Enrique, a high school kid with a faux-hawk who was trying to figure out whether Maria and Dorian were together, or *together*. Maria didn't want to leave (she had just started having fun, and it would be hours before the drugs would wear off), but after some insistence she agreed. Yoshi and his posse laughed at Dorian as he walked out. By not battling, they thought he had admitted defeat.

Afterwards, over a cup of coffee at Mel's Diner (the one in Sherman Oaks, not the one in Hollywood or the one in WeHo), Dorian told Maria the battlers had it all wrong.

"Glowsticking isn't about winning," he said, "it's about art, it's about unity. In most trance songs the music plays at 120 beats per minute. You know why it plays at that particular speed?" Dorian didn't wait for a response. "It's because that's the speed of the human heart as we hear it when we're in our mother's womb. When everyone is listening to the same beat, everyone's thoughts are synchronized, unified, and we can do anything. That's why the government is afraid of raves."

Maria didn't know the government was afraid of raves. She also didn't know multi-variable calculus, or who the Secretary General of the UN was. This last question would later come back to haunt her.

"It's like Falun Gong, in China," Dorian continued. "Even if they don't do anything overtly anti-government, even if they just stretch and meditate, the government is afraid of them, because if one leader can get twenty million people to stretch together, then maybe he can get twenty million people to do other things."

Maria thought about how many people twenty million was. It was a lot of people, she decided, a very large number of people. While the last traces of the ketamine she took at *March Madness* drifted lazily through her veins, she imagined just how many people it would be.

It would be thiiiiiiiiiiiiiiiiiiiiiis many.

In high school, at night, Dorian used to drive girls up to a little stretch of dirt just off of Mulholland Drive. From that spot you can look down and see the entire San Fernando Valley laid out in all of its brilliance. All the buildings looked like little glowsticks. In high school, Dorian would turn the volume of the radio all the way up so he wouldn't have to talk to the girls he brought there. It was a lot easier that way. The girls were only too happy to oblige. They weren't hurt. Usually, they didn't have anything to say anyways.

The night after *March Madness*, Dorian took Maria up to the little stretch of dirt, and he didn't turn the radio on at all. Once the engine was off, Dorian turned to Maria and whispered into her ear in a voice so soft she had to listen just right to hear it, "The Valley at night is the second most beautiful thing in the world."

"That's nice," Maria said. She wondered how long it would take someone to fall to the ground if they jumped.

After an awkward moment of silence, Dorian whispered, "I love you."

"Well, I don't love you," Maria replied, "I don't love anyone, and I never will."

They kissed.

They kissed again after seeing *Dirty Dancing* together at a revival theatre in Northridge at the corner of Tampa and Parthenia (don't bother looking, it's a strip mall now). "Just say the word," said Dorian, "and I'll take you away from all of this. I'll take you wherever you want to go."

Maria found the offer very tempting, but she didn't take him up on it. That night, the Chinese government initiated a crackdown on "Enemy Cults" in the Shanghai area. One hundred and twenty Falun Gong members were arrested over the course of twenty-four hours.

"If I were a glowstick," Dorian told Maria one night on the way home from *Circus Disco*, "I'd be an ultra."

"An ultra?"

"An ultra-high intensity glowstick. Most glowsticks last for eight hours, but ultras, once broken, last only five minutes. One song if you're lucky."

"Why would you want to last for only five minutes?" Maria asked.

"Because for those five minutes, I would be the brightest thing around, a hundred times brighter than any other glowstick in the club. And even after I went out, people would remember that light. They would continue to be affected by whatever that light showed them. What kind of glowstick would you be?"

Maria didn't know. She didn't want to be a glowstick. She wanted to be a penguin.

"What do you want to do when you graduate from college?" Dorian asked.

"I don't know," Maria said. And she meant it, she really didn't. Maria didn't make plans for more than a day in advance, and graduating from college was much, much more than a day in advance.

"Well, I want to join Teach for America," Dorian said, "and teach music and dance to inner city children. Then I want to go to England, and

Palau." Dorian had once read an article about Palau, and even though he forgot what the article was about, he always dreamed of someday going there. "I want to climb to the top of Mt. Whitney, the highest point in California, and shout as loud as I can to see if anyone can hear me. I want to visit the Sistine Chapel and see if it really is beautiful enough to make you cry."

"That's a lot," Maria said. "It would take a lifetime to do all that."

"Well that's what we each have," Dorian smiled. "A lifetime. To spend as best as we can."

"Why do you love me?" Maria asked Dorian one night on the way out of *New Eden*. This was more open than Maria normally was, but DXM tended to do that to her.

"Because," Dorian replied, "you're the most beautiful girl in the world. Not just outside, but inside as well."

Maria wondered what this meant. What did she look like on the inside? Quite slimy, she imagined, slimy and mushy. Like the inside of a pumpkin when you carve it up on Halloween.

"You're a glowstick still in its packaging," Dorian continued, "waiting to be opened, waiting to be snapped. Waiting to light up the world."

It finally went down on April 19th at *New Eden*. Yoshi had sent an e-mail to every contact, posted on every message board, demanding that Dorian face him man to man. Many readers of these statements were aware of the dilemma facing Dorian: if he didn't show up he would be considered a coward, but if he did show up, if he entered the circle and competed with Yoshi, by that very act of competition he would be engaging in the activity he had fought so hard against. He would be giving in to Yoshi's plan. It was Maria's nineteenth birthday.

The crowd was larger than any *New Eden* had seen in years. Dorian and Maria arrived hand in hand, but they separated as soon as they walked in the door. Maria went off to find someone who could sell her ecstasy, while Dorian went to the main dance floor to see Yoshi. There was no sense in delaying the inevitable.

Yoshi was standing by the bar, drink in hand, when Dorian arrived. Several members of his posse, fellow battlers who looked up to him and wanted to someday beat him, were flanking him on either side, but stayed behind as Yoshi stepped forward to greet Dorian.

"I thought you wouldn't come," he said smugly.

"Glowsticking is my passion," Dorian said. "I never decline an invitation to take part in it."

Yoshi gestured to his posse, who dispersed throughout the crowd, letting those in attendance know it was almost time for the main event. The crowd quickly grew quiet, and soon the music died as well. At this cue, Yoshi cleared his throat, and addressed the room.

"Ladies and Gentlemen," Yoshi began, "we are here to determine, once and for all, who is the greatest glowsticker in Los Angeles."

Cheers erupted throughout *New Eden*. Dorian turned to Yoshi. "This is your last chance to back out," Dorian said calmly.

Yoshi laughed in reply. He held up his hands, and lightly pushed Dorian away.

"Let the games begin," Yoshi shouted. Dorian and the other crowd members backed away, giving Yoshi room to work in. Yoshi nodded to the DJ, who started playing Anabolic Frolic's *Pleasure and Pain*.

Yoshi pulled out two glowsticks, one orange and one green, and the room came to life. He was moving this way and that, in and out, every direction at once. His dance was a mixture of ferocious violence and serene beauty. To the crowd, it was as if he had four hands and twice as many glowsticks.

The musical number drew to a close, and Yoshi tossed both glowsticks in the air, catching them smoothly behind his neck. He stepped out of the circle to the sound of applause.

"Your move, hippie," he said to Dorian.

Now it was Dorian's turn. The attendees at the club murmured among themselves, wondering if Dorian would find a way to outdo the magical performance they had just witnessed. Dorian nodded to the DJ booth, and the opening notes to William Orbit's cover of *Adagio for Strings* began to play.

The circle around Dorian expanded even further as he walked slowly to the center. He removed his two trademark aqua glowsticks, one from each pocket, and expertly broke them, shaking them in the same movement so that the chemicals inside began to mix and glow.

Without further ceremony, Dorian placed each glowstick, standing up, in the center of the floor. He stepped backwards and melted into the crowd surrounding the two inert glowsticks.

The crowd was stunned into silence. A murmur of discontent began, but it was quickly silenced. Instead, the entire crowd began to stare at the glowsticks as the music played.

And something magical happened.

Each member of the crowd listened to the music. They truly listened. They let it permeate their innermost being as they stared into the inviting and glowing light at the center of the circle.

Finally the song came to an end, and the spell was broken. In the silence that remained, Dorian stepped forwarded and collected both glowsticks, scooping one into each pocket.

Dorian walked up to Yoshi, who had been stunned into silence just like every other member of the crowd, and put his mouth next to Yoshi's ear so close it looked like he might kiss it. "Do you see now?" he whispered. "It's not about the glowsticker, it's about the glowsticks." And with that Dorian walked away.

It's hard to determine whether this is an historical fact, but anecdotal evidence suggests that Yoshi never glowsticked again.

Maria was fairly oblivious to the world around her whenever she was on ecstasy, especially when she was on ecstasy and leaving the overly bright environment of *New Eden* for the Real World outside. It usually took a few minutes for her senses to adjust to the less-colorful lights of reality, and until they did, everything was like moving through a sepia fog.

This was probably the reason why Maria never saw the truck coming, and never heard the scream of its brakes, but Dorian did. He had just enough time to push Maria out of the way before he became a momentary silhouette against the truck's blinding white lights, his body lit up one final time. The truck driver, an aspiring-screenwriter-turned-aspiring-meth-dealer named Roy, had just started listening to trance music.

Maria was planning to go to the funeral, but when her roommate Blair called to say that Blair's ex-boyfriend Clay (a pre-pre-med at Valley College) had gotten some Percocet from his roommate's mother, it was too good for her to pass up.

While sitting in a chair in her dorm room, Maria fantasized about life as a penguin. What did they do for fun? What did they do for pleasure? Moments before falling to the ground, Maria wondered what would happen if you gave a penguin ecstasy. Would it become even happier?

Freshman year turned into sophomore year (2001 became 2002, and eventually even became 2003). Nights turned into days, wars and politicians came and went. Maria stopped taking ecstasy, and meth, and ketamine, and eventually even DXM. She graduated from USC, spent two years with Teach for America, went to England, went to Palau, climbed Mt. Whitney, saw the Sistine Chapel. And when she had done it all, when she had tried to figure out what to do with her life, how best to spend the time she had been given, she came back to Los Angeles where she belonged.

Glowstickers, real glowstickers, stopped going to *New Eden*. Soon the battlers stopped as well, moving on to some other venue in which to prove their worth to each other and impress the girls. Maria didn't go to *New Eden* anymore either. But on some nights, when her children were put to bed and her husband fell asleep before she did, she would stare at the ceiling, imagining her heart beating at 120 beats per minute while William Orbit played somewhere in the background of her mind. Sometimes, if she listened just right, she could hear Dorian beside her, whispering in her ear, *"If I were a glowstick. . ."*

The Year of 100 Blind Dates

The old man in the worn-out brown sports coat was the only thing standing between me and closing up for the night.

"This place would be a lot more fun to work at if there were no customers," I told Alicia.

Alicia ignored me and focused on the decrepit vending machine in front of her. She smacked the side of it. Hard. Nothing happened. She wound up her meaty arm like a pitcher and smacked it again. This time, a bag of chips clattered down into the collection tray below.

"Without customers, there wouldn't be a library," she said as she bent down.

The old man glanced up at a large clock. He sighed, the gesture shedding dust mites off his old coat and into the air, and struggled to his feet. Step by painful step, he plodded towards the exit.

Alicia straightened, chips in hand. "What's on the menu for tonight? Still re-reading the *Sword of Truth*?"

"I wish. I have a date."

Alicia snorted. "You? A date? Like, with a real person?"

"Is it that hard to believe a girl would go out with me?"

"Do you really want me to answer?"

I shrugged. "Well, my sister set it up. And it's just dinner, I'm not going to a rock concert or anything."

"That would be a sight." She thought for a moment. "How about I close up tonight?"

I raised an eyebrow. "You sure?"

"Absolutely. Wouldn't want you to be late for your... date."

"Thanks, I owe you!"

Before Alicia could change her mind, I ran past the shuffling old man in the worn-out brown sports coat and out the door.

The woman was named Alexa. My sister arranged for me to meet her at Paco's Tacos, a flamboyantly Americanized Mexican restaurant within walking distance of the library. The interior of the restaurant held a dizzying array of primary colors, solid blue tables surrounded by loud red walls. The scent of canned salsa and grease filled the air. The hostess, an oversized sombrero on her head, seated me at a booth towards the back. I was trying to decide between the beef and chicken fajitas when my date arrived.

"Grant, right?"

The woman standing over me had a lean face, cheeks defined by sharp edges. Rows of curly hair fell like a curtain across her shoulders.

Was I supposed to stand up? Hug her? My sister was right, it had been a while. I needed to say something.

"Umm, you must be Alexa."

She held out a hand. "Lexi."

I stared at her hand. One second turned into two. Alexa, or Lexi, pursed her lips. I reached out my own hand, but too late. Lexi was already grasping the table with her previously outstretched hand and sitting down across from me.

So awkward.

"So, come here often?" she asked.

She was pretty enough. I guess. She wore a T-shirt, which seemed a little informal for a first date. The library required us to wear something with a collar. I couldn't see any tattoos, but she gave off an aura like she probably had them. A long and thin gold earring hung from each ear, waving slightly whenever she moved her head.

She stared at me. Oh right, she had asked a question.

I shook my head. "My sister picked the place. She actually set this all up. She said I didn't get out enough, so she made profiles for me on a bunch of dating websites."

Lexi leaned back and crossed her arms. "You didn't write your profile?"

"Not one word."

Her eyes let loose an interrogating glare. "So you're not actually into rockabilly?"

"Is he on MTV?"

Lexi brushed her hair behind one ear and exhaled. "Well, what kind of music do you listen to?"

"None, really." I dropped my gaze. "I'm not a music person."

Our waiter, a teenager with an absurd peach fuzz mustache perched on his upper lip, interrupted. "Can I get you something to drink?"

Without taking her eyes off me, Lexi handed him the menu. "Diet coke. Combo number one."

The waiter nodded. "And you, sir?"

That's right, I hadn't decided what to get. Chicken or steak. It was decision time. Now or never.

"So, the thing is," I rubbed the crease of the menu with my thumb. "I like fajitas, and I'm trying to decide between steak or chicken. Which one is more, like, fajita-ish?"

The waiter cleared his throat. "Umm. Both?"

"Well then." Deep breath in, deep breath out. "I guess, I'll—"

"He'll have the steak." Lexi plucked the menu out of my hands and thrust it at the waiter.

The waiter ducked away from our booth.

My face burned. "What did you do that for?"

"Not a music person?" Lexi scoffed. "There isn't *any* music you like? Any?"

"I read a lot. It's hard to read with music playing."

Lexi just stared.

"I like epic fantasy. I usually read series. But if a new book comes out, and it's been a while since the last one, I have to re-read the previous books. Like, Ken Scholes just finished the last book in the *Psalms of Isaak*, but it's been six years since I read book four, so now I'm going to have to re-read all the previous books."

Lexi folded her hands, closed her eyes for a moment, then opened them. "That is literally the stupidest thing I have ever heard."

The low wail of a siren shattered the moment. I cocked my ear. It was coming from the table next to us. And it wasn't a normal siren, more like an air raid siren from a war movie. The same siren sounded again, this time from another table, then from another. Then from both of our pockets.

Just like that, I recognized the sound. The citywide public emergency app. I looked down at my phone.

"*Warning,*" the message began. "*Increased novel virus strains have been detected in your area. Please be advised, Level Four lockdown is now in effect for all areas within city limits.*"

Lexi stared at her phone. "What on earth?"

The last time there was a virus outbreak, we never went beyond Level Three. I couldn't even remember what Level Four meant.

Another siren. Another message. My unasked question was answered.

"*Level Four Lockdown restrictions are as follows: All citizens are required to refrain from visiting any location outside their place of residence. Exceptions are provided for any location visited by that citizen in the last twelve hours. Message over.*"

Lexi slammed her phone down on the table. "They've got to be kidding. That makes no sense."

I gulped. "Well, the idea is that if you were around anyone in the last twelve hours who had the virus, you've already been exposed. So, as long as you only go places—"

"I understand *why* they're doing it." Lexi threw back her head and sucked air through clenched teeth. "Argh. I have a concert tomorrow night."

"You're going to a concert?"

"Playing a concert. Guitar. At Mystic Coffee, downtown. Thirty-eight open mic nights, and finally they said I could do my own concert. My one chance, and now…"

I exhaled. "Since you didn't go there today, you can't go there tomorrow."

Lexi glared. "No kidding, bookworm."

Alicia was already at the circulation desk when I arrived at work the next morning, scanning in the returned books from the overnight drop box.

"I know I don't work on Saturdays," she said. "But I was reading the lockdown rules, and since I came here yesterday, I didn't know if that meant I had to come here again today."

I grabbed a handful of books and started scanning them at my station. "I don't think you have to come in. I mean, you're allowed to stay home if you want. You just can't go anywhere you didn't go yesterday."

Alicia paused mid-scan. "This is the only place I went yesterday. Nowhere else." Her station beeped impatiently, waiting for the next book. "Joey, my son, he was with Rick all day yesterday. I was supposed to pick him up after work, but I was so tired I asked Rick if he could keep him an extra night. And now…"

I looked down at my shoes. "Well, I'm sure the lockdown won't last long."

Alicia exhaled. "Yeah, you're probably right."

We finished scanning the books in silence.

When I arrived at Paco's Tacos that night, Lexi was already at our booth from the night before. The air smelled like someone had left the deep fryer uncovered all night.

"I didn't know if you'd come," I said.

"Well, it was either this or ramen at home, seeing as this is the only restaurant I went to yesterday, and thus the only restaurant I'll be allowed to visit for the rest of all time."

I sat down. "Well, it's just until the lockdown is lifted."

Lexi snorted. "So, second blind date," she said, reviewing the menu. "You get a lot of those?"

"No. First one."

The same waiter as the night before, ridiculous moustache still clinging to his upper lip for dear life, cleared his throat.

I looked down at the closed menu. "Do I have to get steak fajitas? Since I ordered them yesterday?"

The waiter swallowed and looked over his shoulder. "I think? Just in case someone's, you know, watching."

"Combo two," Lexi declared, closing the menu and pushing it across the table towards the waiter.

"That's not what she got last night," I whispered to the waiter.

"I know it's not what I got last night," Lexi shouted. "It doesn't matter. The lockdown doesn't mean we have to eat the same thing every night. That's ridiculous."

The waiter backed away from the table.

"Why are you so pissy?" I asked.

Lexi threw out her hands. "I'm supposed to be playing a concert right now."

"Well I'm supposed to be reading a book right now."

"Then read a book." Lexi drew out each syllable. "I'm missing out on my big break, and you're upset that you aren't reading? You could read anywhere, anytime you want. Just do it."

So, on our third blind date, I brought *Faith of the Fallen* by Terry Goodkind to read.

Lexi raised her right eyebrow so high I thought it would fly off her face. "You're seriously going to sit there and read while we eat dinner?"

I kept reading.

On our sixth blind date, I got to try the chicken fajitas.

"The usual," I told the waiter.

He shuffled his feet. "About that, sir. We're out of steak."

"Am I allowed to change my order?"

"Allowed to?" Lexi was trying to balance a spoon from her nose. "You are literally the most boring person on earth. How am I stuck in a time loop episode with you?"

The morning after our eighteenth blind date, I closed up the library for good. Alicia stopped showing up to work after day five, as did the other circulation assistants. A few customers, of course only the ones who had come on that last day of normalcy, continued to poke their heads in from time to time, but it slowed to a trickle. The old man in the worn-out brown sports coat never showed up. Maybe the virus got him.

After three consecutive days of no customers, and no other staff, I closed it up for good. I took a stack of books I still needed to read, carefully checked them out to myself one by one, then set out for Paco's.

For our twenty-sixth date we pretended to be each other. I can't remember how we got the idea. I talked with my nose thrust into the air and ordered a random combo off the menu.

Lexi brought a copy of *Blue Like Jazz*, which she said was the only book she owned. She wore fake thick rimmed glasses, empty frames with no lenses, and kept pushing them up on her nose.

"I don't even wear glasses," I protested.

Lexi whined, "I don't even wear glasses."

"I sound nothing like that," I tried to say, but dissolved into laughter before I could finish.

On our fifty-eighth date, we dressed up like we were going to prom. I let slip to Lexi on our forty-ninth date that I didn't go to mine, so she said we should fix that. I wore a shirt and tie with an old suit jacket, while Lexi wore an ugly pink bridesmaid dress. Whenever the waiter walked by, we loudly voiced our fears to each other that he would check our IDs. He was not amused.

On our seventy-fifth date, the restaurant ran out of everything but chips. The waiter said something about supply chain issues. We didn't care. Starting that night, we still ordered our usuals, even though chips were all we got.

Lexi would pretend to get angry at the waiter. "I said red enchiladas—these are green," gesturing at the handful of chips on her plate. "Send it back."

On our ninety-eighth date, Paco's Tacos closed. For a full week, we had been the only customers. I never knew what happened to the others. Maybe they were afraid of the virus. Maybe they had died of the virus. Or, maybe they just got sick of eating only chips.

"This is our last night open," the waiter said. "Most of the staff have left, and the rest of us, we just don't see the point in continuing."

After the waiter's announcement, Lexi barely ate her chips. I brought up topics to needle her, like how there's no difference between folk music and emo music, but she would just stare to the side. When we left, we both stood outside the restaurant.

I spoke first. "So, should we check out a different restaurant tomorrow?"

Lexi crossed her arms. "It's not funny."

"Come on, yes it is."

No response.

"Look," I said. "I'm just trying to make the best of the situation. I mean, what do you suggest we do?"

"I'm going home." Lexi began to walk down the street.

"But what about tomorrow night?"

Lexi flicked her hand without turning around. "Do whatever you want, bookworm."

After I could no longer see her receding figure in the distance, I turned the other way and went home.

The next night, there was a firm knock on my apartment door. When I opened it, Lexi stood on the other side, guitar case strapped to her back.

"May I?"

I nodded. She made her way into the living room.

Her eyes widened. Custom wooden shelves covered every inch of the wall from the worn carpet to the popcorn ceiling. The various shelves, precisely labeled, were divided into every possible sub-genre of fantasy and science-fiction. Separating high fantasy from urban fantasy, or space opera from alternate universe fiction, made certain shelving decisions difficult (how do you classify the *Pern* series?), but it created an order that I just couldn't live without. Only when every book was in its proper place could I possibly feel at peace.

"You've got a lot of books," Lexi finally said.

I smiled. "I'm a librarian. They're kind of my life."

Lexi removed the guitar case from behind her back. She opened the case and pulled out the guitar with surgical delicacy. Without explanation, she began to play.

At first she plucked individual strings, ringing out discordant notes one at a time, keeping me guessing at when a note would next appear. It was like raindrops falling on a window during the first moments of a storm. Then the notes resolved into a rhythm. There was body, structure, something approaching a melody. Her mouth was silent, the guitar itself the only voice. She strummed low chords, creating a foundation, then interspersed individual high notes. In my mind I saw dolphins jumping out of a calm ocean, then stars plunging out of the sky. People being born, living, dying, falling in and out of love, laughing and crying. The notes wove a tapestry in front of my eyes.

Mid-note, she stopped.

I exhaled, realizing for the first time that I had been holding my breath. "That was beautiful."

Lexi looked down at me. She deposited the guitar back in its case.

"I'm leaving," she said.

"You can come back again tomorrow night."

She closed the case with a thud. "No, I'm leaving the city."

I furrowed my brow. "Where are you going?"

"Somewhere."

"Somewhere?"

"Before the internet went out, I read rumors about people forming communities in the mountains. Self-sufficient farms, like homesteaders in the old days." The guitar case clasps shut.

"So you're going to go, what, be a farmer out in the mountains?"

Lexi put the case back on her back and walked to the door. She opened it. Paused for a moment.

"Will you come with me?" she asked, not turning around.

I remained seated. The images from her song still played across my imagination. But then, they began to fade.

"I need to finish the *Shannara* series," I said. "I'm almost done. Just two books left."

Even though I couldn't see them I knew Lexi was rolling her eyes. "See you later, bookworm."

And with that, she was gone.

After Lexi left, the nights got louder. During the day I could read for hours without disturbance. But at night, outside voices pierced the walls of my apartment, filling it up like a cloud of poison gas.

One night, the voices were so loud it sounded like there was a rave outside my building. I had to see what was going on. For the first time since Lexi left, I pulled my shoes out of the wardrobe and put them on. I grabbed an old sweatshirt and dragged it over my head in case it was cold outside. With a deep breath, I opened my apartment door.

Every light in the hallway was either dead or flickering. Discarded bags of trash leaned against walls like drunks at a bar. A jagged gash ran through the carpet starting in front of the unit next to mine. I almost turned around, but pressed on.

The street outside was a mix between a block party and the end of the world. Screaming people were everywhere. Sirens mingled with the distinct percussion of breaking glass. A street preacher with an unkempt beard yelled into a megaphone. An old man poured gasoline on a mailbox, an eager lighter in his hand. The smell of smoke, accompanied by other more bitter smells, filled my nostrils.

"You!"

I turned towards a faceless police officer, any distinguishing features hidden behind an opaque face shield.

"Back off." He pointed at me with his baton.

"But I live here," I started to say.

"I won't say it again, back off!"

A form racing down the street slammed into the police officer, knocking him onto the ground. I turned and ran, back into my building, back into my apartment, and locked the door.

I resolved to stay inside after that, and I did. Until I ran out of food. And, more importantly, out of books. That's what led me, one morning, to set out to the one place where I could find more of both.

I made the trek to the library during the day, when things were quietest. I didn't encounter another living person during the trip. No movement at all, just burnt husks of cars and busted in storefronts.

The inside of the library was pristine, untouched by the violence outside its doors. A little dusty, but otherwise no worse for the wear.

Days became weeks, and weeks became months. I slept on the couches in the children's section. I emptied the vending machines. I read every book I ever wanted to, but hadn't had the time to truly savor and enjoy.

That's how I lived my life. Until the day Lexi came back.

"I thought I'd find you here."

Her face glowed, as if powered by some inner light. She looked more at ease than she had during our ninety-eight dinners at Paco's Tacos.

"I found a community in the mountains," she told me. "It's about a week's walk away. They're starting to rebuild. They have a greenhouse, a chicken coop." She surveyed the shelves around us. "No library though."

My face reddened. The shelves were dustier than ever. I should have cleaned them, would have if I had known I would have company.

I cleared my throat. "Do you still play music?"

Lexi's grin filled her entire face. "Of course. At night, after the chores are finished, we build a fire. A real no kidding fire. We sit around, just talking. If the mood strikes, I play."

"So, why did you come back then?"

Lexi chuckled. "For you. Like I said, the community doesn't have a library."

"I thought you didn't read." I looked down at my shoes.

She flashed a true smile, no hint of sarcasm, warmer and more genuine than any I had ever seen before. "I figured the new world needs both books and music."

I fingered the last few pages of the book I had been reading. "I wouldn't be much use."

"I think you'd be surprised. Sure, it's a lot of work. Probably more work than you've ever done in your life. But if I learned to do it, you can too."

She reached out her hand, just like she did a year ago when we first met. That outstretched hand filled my entire field of vision. Until I looked down at the book in my hands. *Hymn* by Ken Scholes.

"I'm sorry. I can't. I have just a few pages left." I gestured at the shelves surrounding me. "And after that, there are just so many other books. You know?"

Lexi opened her mouth as if to make a final plea, then closed it and shook her head. She exhaled. "Well, see you later. Bookworm."

"Later."

She turned and walked away. The door slammed behind her, echoing throughout the empty library.

I studied the cover of my book. *Hymn*. The final book of the series. Just a few pages left, and I would finally know how it ends.

The book snapped shut. I chucked it at a shelving cart, missed by several feet, then ran out the door and down the deserted street, chasing Lexi's receding figure in the distance.

About the Author

J.B. Masaji is originally from Los Angeles, but now lives in El Paso, Texas with his wife and two children. He is the author of one novel and several short stories. Everything he does is by the grace of God.

jbmasaji@gmail.com

Made in the USA
Middletown, DE
29 May 2023

31099756R00073